The Keepers of Echowah

A NOVEL

TO: Jim

Sonny Sammons

Sonny Sammons

7-31-99

CHEROKEE PUBLISHING COMPANY
ATLANTA, GEORGIA
1995

Library of Congress Cataloging-in-Publication Data

Sammons, Sonny, 1942–
    The Keepers of Echowah/ Sonny Sammons. —1st ed.
        p. cm.
        ISBN 0-87797-269-9 : $17.95 (est.)
        1. Plantation life—Georgia—Fiction. 2. Family—Georgia—
Fiction. 3. Boys—Georgia—Fiction. I. Title.
PS3569.A4657028 1994
813'.54—DC20   94-29932
                                                        CIP

Copyright © 1995 by John William Sammons, Jr.

This book is printed on acid-free paper which conforms to the American National Standard Z39.48-1984 *Permanence of Paper for Printed Library Materials.* Paper that conforms to this standard's requirements for pH, alkaline reserve and freedom from ground-wood is anticipated to last several hundred years without significant deterioration under normal library use and storage conditions.

This book is a work of fiction. Names, characters, places, and incidents either are products of the author's imagination or are used fictitiously. Any resemblance to actual events or locales or persons, living or dead, is entirely coincidental.

Manufactured in the United States of America
First Edition
ISBN: 0-87797-269-9

01   00   99   98   97   96   95   10   9   8   7   6   5   4   3   2

Edited by Alexa Selph
Book design and cover design by Lee-Ann B. Williams
Cover illustration by Taiyo Hasegawa

 Cherokee Publishing Company
P.O. Box 1730, Marietta, GA 30061

Prologue

My entire life I've been convinced that the Lord, even though infinitely wise and omnipotent, probably experienced fleeting interludes of moods more mundane than ethereal, and at these times he decided to create a very special place of absolute beauty for his own private enjoyment, or just for the times when he merely needed to quietly reflect, or when he might have been blue or lonely. Because the nature of omnipotence is to share what is good and grand, I believe that he then chose a very special few to live in, work in, and to share this special place. I believe that I was among the ranks of the chosen.

When first I became old enough to sense the splendor of the land I lived in or to breathe the heady smell of ripening cotton or fresh-plowed earth, or any of the thousands of other sensations that taunted and teased a young boy's senses, I became even more certain that God had picked me to be one of the chosen few. The delicious loneliness of sitting by a pristine beaver pond in late afternoons and hearing the chilling call of a whippoorwill searching the last rays of sun for its mate, made even a child of my young age reflect with a clarity far more mature and knowledgeable than should be allowed.

My earliest memories are of mornings of unsurpassed brilliance and beauty, with skies blue as robins' eggs. The days would end in sunsets as red as if all the flames of hell and all the fires of the primordial beginning had meshed into one show of light. I believed that every single sensation, no matter how small, was created solely for my own personal satisfaction. The aroma of full-bloom honeysuckle in late summer could leave a young boy of blossoming puberty dizzy with feelings and emotions he wasn't quite ready to understand yet, but that he knew, in his rapidly maturing mind and body, would soon and surely be revealed to him.

It was a time when a young boy could sneak his father's old single-barreled shotgun (without the shells because he didn't want to piss God off by killing one of his creatures) and whistle for the old lemon-colored pointer sleeping under the house and wander off among the pines and blackberry patches. When the old dog locked down in an absolutely perfect point, with his tail high and quivering, and ten excited quail burst from their cover, at that moment my heart would get stuck in my throat. Walking home later, when the red sun was twice its normal size in the west and a full moon lay orange as a pumpkin in the eastern sky, and I caught the sight of a perfect vee of southbound geese against a purple sky, then I was absolutely convinced that the place in which I lived was the place that the Lord had chosen as his favorite.

My twin brother, Patty, would have explained the phenomenon far more explicitly than I. He probably would have said, "Boy, Matty, if I owed somebody a pretty place and they wouldn't take this place as payment, I'd cancel the fucking debt. If this isn't the prettiest place on earth, there ain't a pine tree in Maine or a cow in Texas. If somebody came to south Georgia and didn't think it was the greatest place on earth, I'd have that son of a bitch sent to the mental ward at the state hospital and put under shotgun guard. Just getting up in the mornings down here will make your dick hard."

CHAPTER 1

In the Beginning

PATTY WAS BORN FIVE MINUTES EARLIER AND seven ounces heavier than me, and he immediately assumed an attitude of primogeniture that took me years to overcome. Our birth was simultaneous with our mother's death, and from that day forward I think our father blamed Patty and me for the loss of his wife. This was October 17, 1944. St. Louis had won the World Series the day before. Within the next two weeks Roosevelt and Truman would reduce Dewey and Bricker to the ranks of the unemployed. The International Red Cross had won the Nobel Peace Prize, and a beautiful young girl named Bess Myerson became Miss America. Joe Louis was heavyweight champion of the world, and the country had the memory of Pearl Harbor and almost three horrible years of war to add to its history books. When the doctor told our father that our mother was dead, he left the hospital and no one saw him for three weeks. The hospital was overcrowded with America's finest, returning home with missing limbs or hearts or minds, and its administrators were not inclined to take on two screaming children whose own father didn't care whether they lived or died.

The hospital director called the plantation where my father worked, but no one there had seen him. Someone on the plantation located my mother's brother, Uncle Charlie Anderson, in Memphis, Tennessee. Two hours later he had settled his monthly account at the Peabody Hotel and packed his belongings, which were few because he lived at the hotel. Daybreak found Uncle Charlie in southern Tennessee, and twenty-four hours after he left his beloved Peabody, a big black Mark I Continental Cabriolet sat idling in the emergency lane of the hospital. Uncle Charlie had arrived.

Uncle Charlie was a big man and ruggedly handsome. To those who met him for the first time, he evoked the mental image of the Old West or a riverboat gambler. He was a flamboyant enigma. Age and an old football injury had kept him from being drafted into the army, but when he burst through the front doors of the hospital demanding to see "the fellow in charge," every nurse's eyes swarmed over his face and the bulges in his pants like honeybees over wildflowers on a warm spring day.

He immediately took charge, filled out the birth certificates, named my brother James Patrick (for my father's father), named me John Matthew (for my mother's), and paid the bill, openly flirting with the pretty nurses all the while. He nicknamed us Patty and Matty, and drove us to the house at the crossroads where he had waited so proudly five years ago and listened to the bent and gray country preacher who wedded his frail little sister to Gus MacDonald. This would be where we were to live for the next seventeen years.

Uncle Charlie's intention was to bring us to the plantation where my father was employed and to leave us. He figured he could be back in Memphis in time for the poker game on Thursday night. He woke my father, who had been drunk for three weeks. "Gus, you want to tell me what the hell is going on?"

"She's dead. The doctor told her when she got pregnant that she was committing suicide."

Uncle Charlie looked deep into his eyes and saw something that made him forget about the poker game on Thursday. "Well, she left something behind. I brought them home. I'll be staying here until I feel confident that my baby sister's children will be adequately taken care of. Now I ain't going to stay here with you smelling the way you are, so you and me might as well get some things straightened out right now before this turns into an altercation involving pistols."

"She was too gentle a person for me, Charlie. She was more than any man deserved."

"I know. She even made pets out of the bumblebees."

My father found a way to ease his pain a short while later, leaving me and Patty orphaned, and Uncle Charlie stayed the rest of his life. Why he did it, I'll never know. He gave up a life of reading poker faces and figuring the odds of catching the card he needed from the remainder of an undealt deck. He had lived in the best hotel in Memphis, played seven-card stud four nights a week, fought game chickens on Sundays, and took his vacations at the horse tracks in Saratoga Springs or Miami. He probably had more women in his life than Errol Flynn, and he traded them for a life in a five-room frame house in southwest Georgia, tending two little kids that made bad smells in their clothes. Sometimes in the middle of the night, when the wind whistled through the cracks in the old house and it was freezing cold, he would come into our room to be sure we were covered and warm, or he would feel our foreheads to see if we were catching a cold or had a fever, or he would just stand there in the night looking at us with a strange smile on his face.

Uncle Charlie was the type of man everyone instantly

liked and admired. He was a man's man, and I thought that even the local undertaker would be sorry when he died. He could be hard as flint, if the occasion called for it, or he could be as soft as the misty fog of late October. He would, one instant, curse like a drunken sailor, and the next would quote biblical scripture or entire passages from the works of Shakespeare. His solutions to problems and difficulties were usually solved with the wisdom of Solomon, but with a Tennessee drawl. When I was small I once heard him arguing with a foxhunting buddy about the pedigree of a Walker hound he was considering buying from the man. "He looks like a pretty good dog, and he's got the right colors and fine muscling, but I'm not going to risk my money until I hear the dog hunt."

The other hunter replied, "Charlie, that dog's daddy won the North Carolina state championship last year, you know damn well the dog will hunt, and besides that I need the money."

"Lem," Uncle Charlie answered, "that might well be so, but to me it's just like that big old bell in the steeple at St. Joseph. It looked like a bell to me and it was the color of a bell and it's hung in the right place to be a bell and it's even got a pull rope like all the bells I've ever seen's got, but until I heard that son of a bitch ring I couldn't swear that it was a bell."

Thank the Lord Uncle Charlie didn't raise us completely by himself. Aunt Hattie played a big part. She was the finest, most noble woman on the face of the earth. She was hard as nails in her convictions, but in spirit she was as gentle as an angel's breath. She was black, born and raised on the plantation, and believed in "haints, and spooks, magical spells, and hexes." She practiced white magic, and could remove hexes if the victim got to her in time. Most of the blacks and some of the white people on the plantation wore her little strange-smelling asafetida bags tied on thongs around their necks to ward off the vapors or hellfire hexes. She said that her grandparents were born as slaves on this land. She was old when Patty and I were born, and thank goodness she kept getting older. Everyone called on Aunt Hattie for remedies to cure everything from warts to broken hearts. Uncle Charlie even tried to get her to cast spells on his game-cocks. She didn't.

When they found my father's pickup truck wrapped around the abutment of a concrete bridge two months after we were born, Aunt Hattie flitted to our house like a great purple butterfly, fussing and grumbling about "the biggest mess I ever seen," and ordered Uncle Charlie to get out of the house and let a woman take care of these children for a while. We never enjoyed the luxury of dirt between our toes at bedtime from that day forth.

As Uncle Charlie was leaving the house, she stopped

him. "You know Colonel O'Hearn is off at the war and he can't tell us his wishes. The menfolks got together and voted for you to be the manager till the Colonel comes home."

CHAPTER 2

Echowah

HOME FOR PATTY AND ME WAS A SHOOTING PLANTATION IN South Georgia. It was dedicated almost exclusively to the hedonistic pleasures of wealthy industrialists, powerful politicians, or the idle rich. But not quite. The Internal Revenue Service code required that in order to qualify as a tax deduction, the so-called farm had to have income that offset, or almost offset, expenditures. Consequently, hunting plantations either developed a customer base and hunted for compensation, or they truly tried to make a profit with a row crop operation. My father had been employed here as plantation manager. Because of the plantation owner's military background and his present business relationship with the U.S. government, he demanded that the plantation not only foot the bill for the hedonism; he wanted it to actually pay taxes, too. The fact that the farming entity of the plantation managed to do just that, year after year, was a tribute to the hard-working people on the plantation that too often went unnoticed. After World War II the owner retired from the army as a war-hardened colonel, and praise for a job well done was not in his vocabulary.

Original plantation properties in Georgia were usually obtained under a land grant from the King of England at the time when Georgia had been a colony. The ones not ceded by land grant were bought, fee simple, for a few pennies an acre. The only criterion for land to be titled as a plantation was that it must contain at least eight hundred acres in one contiguous tract. Originally, all of these farms were working plantations. Cotton was planted for the cash crop and feed grains were grown for the mules and other livestock. Each plantation, out of necessity, was a microcosm of a self-sustaining and self-governing economic system. Only the exotics such as coffee, tea, and silks for the ladies were not produced on the farm. Each plantation raised and processed almost one hundred percent of its needs, and each one usually had its own commissary and even issued its own scrip for purchasing. Originally worked with slave labor, then with freed labor, most places maintained their status or grew in size by annexing adjoining properties, and they either flourished or suffered according to whims of nature and the weather, or the price of cotton.

When the boll weevil jumped the Rio Grande and invaded Texas in the early 1890s, a flurry of debate ensued in Georgia among the landowners as to the likelihood that the insect would ever reach this far east. The general consensus was that the mighty Mississippi River would forever contain the ruinous little bastard to lands west. When news reached Georgia that the insect had crossed the Mississippi River in 1907, had invaded Louisiana, then Mississippi, and had done to their economies what Sherman had done without firing a shot, the believers prayed, and the cynics dug shallow trenches around their fields and put arsenic in them. The Chattahoochee River didn't stop the boll weevil either, and shortly thereafter King Cotton was dethroned.

The southwestern portion of the state of Georgia, particularly around Thomasville and Albany, was so well adapted to the bobwhite quail, which the boll weevil didn't affect, that when the financially strapped cotton farmers had to sell, rich Yankees were there to buy and to turn the lands into hunting preserves.

Many hunting plantations were named by reversing the owners' last names. For example, Olin would become Nilo Plantation, or Hanes would become Senah Plantation. Many of the plantations were named for Indian place names or Indian words. We lived on Echowah Plantation, "Echowah" being the Muskogean Creek Indian word for "where sleeping deer lie." The Creek tribe indigenous to the area of our plantation was held in particular esteem by the man who had owned the land when it was named.

In the War of 1812, the Creek Indian nation was armed, equipped, and goaded into an uprising against Americans by the British. "Old Hickory" (Andrew Jackson) was sent to Georgia and Alabama to deal with the uprising. Only the Creek tribe that lived in our area and the Talladega tribe, which was then at present-day Talladega, Alabama, sided with the Americans. When Jackson got to the Talladega River and found a cooperative and friendly Creek tribe, he welcomed their friendship and, using their knowledge of the terrain and any other information they could provide, he formed the famous "crescent of death, circle of death." He sent nine scouts toward unfriendly Creek encampments to the south, while he positioned his army around a well-hidden crescent. When the provoked Indians pursued the scouts into the valley, Jackson completed the circle and lost six men while the Creeks lost hundreds. Jackson was considered a hero.

My personal feelings were that what the American

military did to the Indian people made Sherman look like Mary Poppins in comparison.

When I was a young boy I told my Uncle Charlie how I felt.

"Matty," he said, "you talk like you ain't got a lick of sense. We stole this land, fair and square, from them Indians. Besides that, I don't know any self-respecting Indian who would want this land back, after the mess we've made of it." Then gentler, to let me know he wasn't serious and felt the same as I, he would say, "Matty, June second, 1924, Congress granted citizenship to all the Indians in America. If I had been in Congress I would have asked their permission to live here and to grant citizenship to us."

Echowah Plantation contained fifteen thousand acres and was owned by a wealthy Yankee industrialist and ex-army colonel named O'Hearn. The Colonel inherited the plantation and control of a large complex of industrial factories from his family, and his client base ranged from Pentagon bigwigs to movie production people. We never knew if his next guests' occupations would be generals, automobile manufacturing executives, or movie makers. Sometimes we were pleasantly surprised by the guests' genteel manners and their unpretentious ways. Invariably these guests tipped the plantation staff generously when they left. Usually, though, the guests' manners were not quite as august. These people either showed indifferent aloofness toward the people who waited their needs, or they displayed a disdain that camouflaged their own insecurities. We could read them with almost absolute accuracy. The big tippers were magnates, owners, generals, presidents of companies, head honchos, top cheeses, people the mountain came to. The indifferent and aloof people were company vice-presidents, climbers, and back stabbers, people who thought they should be where the buck stopped. The people openly displaying disdain were usually purchasing agents.

The plantation was maintained to botanical-garden standards with a cadre of full-time gardeners, supplemented by field hands not busy with the crops. The dog boys (i.e., Patty and I) could also be seen with a goosenecked hoe in our hands whenever they could catch us. The sole exemptions from gardening were the horse and dog trainers, the hunting guides, and, of course, the kitchen and house staff.

The main house was tremendous and imposing. It was centered at the end of a two-mile-long, perfectly straight sand road. Canopied by large live oaks draped with witches' tresses of Spanish moss, the road on dark nights would assume an eerie and ghostly quality. When Patty and I were children we would double-dog-dare each other to walk to the end and back on moonless nights. Invariably, a gentle wind would whisper through the pines or rustle the leaves and make the long tresses of moss ghost-dance or sway. We never once made it to the end of the road, and we never actually walked back. The main house had an energy all its own.

If they could have spoken, the graceful branches of the wide live oaks that girded the house could have laid claim to having shaded and witnessed the peaceful gatherings of the Chickasaw chief and the tall man who built the house. They had witnessed the two—one red, one white—greet and sit and smoke the pipe of peace as the maidens danced the Dance of the Sun. They stood guard in a gentle rain and nodded their approval as the tall white man took for a bride the chief's daughter, first in a ceremony that the deity of the red man blessed, then with the traditional vows of the white man's presbytery. Three decades later the ancient sentinels watched gallant gray-clad young men, farm boys turned warriors, from a hastily formed company, mount up and follow Captain O'Hearn north to put the Damn Yankee in his place. And four years later they wept with the old men who rested under their shade as a mere twenty of the original two hundred hobbled by with heads held high. Farm boys turned warriors, farm boys turned angels. For untold nights and an equal number of days, from the dew of dawn until the whippoorwills called, the big oaks shaded and sheltered.

The main house was built in the 1830s by German craftsmen. Georgian architecture prevailed, but hints of the romanesque were evidenced by the graceful arches and bays and the diametrically opposed twin staircases that swept a curving arch from the first floor to a confluence on the second. If Margaret Mitchell had seen this setting prior to 1936, Rhett Butler would surely have said, "Frankly, my dear, I don't give a damn," in southwest Georgia. The second floor of the house was my favorite. This was where diplomats, harlots, generals, kings, and literally thousands of captains of commerce had slept, and I knew that whatever it took, someday I would sleep there, also.

Each room on the bottom floor had its own theme. The library walls and doors were raised panel walnut, and the door and cabinet hardware and light fixtures were sterling silver. The space from the picture rail to the pressed-tin ceiling was papered in silk with a floral design. Oil paintings of English fox hunts embellished the walls. The giant dining room was wainscoted from the floor to the chair rail with first-growth, long-leaf, yellow pine. The entire wall from the wainscoting to the ceiling had served as a giant canvas for a Native American hunting scene.

The dark-skinned braves looked almost lifelike as they stalked the white-tailed deer on the opposite wall. Each bedroom upstairs was named for a different color, and all the accoutrements within were that color. The blue bedroom was my favorite. When the Colonel had guests, he always stayed in a small apartment built onto the stables and connected to the main house by a boxwood-lined path of river gravel that hurt your feet when you were barefoot and made loud crunching sounds when you had on shoes. The only noticeable changes made to the house since it was built were basic modernizations such as plumbing and electricity. Meticulous care was always taken not to alter the original structure in any way.

Eight grassfree paths, each lined with liriope, flame of the woods, moss rose, native violets and other ground cover that I couldn't readily identify, meandered like octopus arms from the house to eight gardens. Lesser paths broke from the main paths occasionally and led to the giant live oaks, where white-slatted benches girded their trunks like latticework necklaces. Each garden had its own flavor. The Japanese garden had a rock-lined pool inhabited by golden carp that flitted in and out of the shadows of a half-moon foot bridge, or dodged the Egyptian white lotus and pickerelweed that dotted the surface of the pool. The rose garden was my favorite. When the roses were in full bloom and I was a child, I would dart from one bush to the next, stuffing my nose into each bloom like a giant and wingless earthbound bee, never contenting myself as to which one pleased my senses the most.

On warm spring days when I was growing up, I would often slip away from whatever chore I had been assigned and go to my favorite hiding place. I would lie on the soft grass at the base of a tall pine with just enough canopy to block the sun but not enough to obstruct my view of the sky and clouds. Scattered clumps of broomsedge ensured that I not be seen. I would lie there for hours in the warm spring sunshine listening to the bluetail flies droning, watching a red-tailed hawk or Mississippi kite riding thermals while looking for their supper, and daydreaming of owning the plantation. I saw myself riding the fields astride a white Arabian stallion, dressed in high-topped riding boots with jodhpurs tucked in. A wide-brimmed hat set at a rakish angle and an ever-present riding crop were always a part of my ensemble. I would be the boss, the big cheese, "the goddam sergeant general," and I would never, ever clean the dog shit out of the kennels again.

The old frame house we lived in was located in the northwest part of the plantation at the corner of a crossroads. Looking from above, the house was perfectly square with a pointed tin roof. Wide porches spanned three sides and played host to the large rocking chairs that were ever present on southern porches. The porch slanted ever so slightly to ensure that a blowing rain would find a more accommodating resting place. When Patty and I were small boys we would start next to the weatherboard wall and feverishly rock, inching slowly toward the five-foot-high edge of the porch. He always stopped his chair with one-third of the rocker protruding over the edge. On more than one occasion me and my chair would travel an extra five feet vertically. Patty and I lived and grew up here, mostly unsupervised and often neglected; we were told what to do but rarely talked to. And so we grew with unchecked leaps toward manhood, never looking back, or even to the side, for impending danger.

CHAPTER 3

Kerosene and Turpentine

S AM HOUSTON JONES WAS MY MULE-BRAINED FIRST COUSIN on my mother's side of the family. He was born in the Great State of Texas; his father was born in the Great State, his grandfather, great-grandfather, and great-great-grandfather were born in the Great State, and I sometimes wished that the border between the United States and Mexico had been set at the Mississippi River instead of the Rio Grande. Sam Houston's mother was my mother's older sister. Aunt Mary was born two years after my Uncle Charlie Anderson and eight years before my deceased mother. My aunt was a mousy woman, totally subservient to my Uncle Laurice, and overly doting on her only child, Sam Houston.

Sam Houston (his father called him S.H., his mother

called him Sammie, and Patty called him Shithead) was one year older than Patty and me. He was big, unbelievably ugly, had an I.Q. lower than most high school football scores, and his great-great-great-grandfather fought against Santa Anna in the glorious liberation of Texas. His folks brought him to South Georgia and left him for the summer each year from the time he was five years old until he got big enough and could beat up my Uncle Laurice, and Uncle Laurice told the same damned story every year in the interim. I think first cousins must marry each other a lot in Texas. The gene pool is mighty weak. Might even need draining.

Patty said it was a matter of evolution. He said the entire Jones family hadn't too long ago climbed down out of the trees.

My Uncle Laurice would start his story, "Now, boys, your cousin, Sam Houston here, was named after the 'Great One' himself, a man my great-great-granddaddy fought tooth and nail by. I remember my granddaddy telling me this story like it was yesterday. You boys listening?"

Patty would yawn and say, "Uncle Laurice you told us this story last year." I would say, "Yes, sir."

"Anyhow, Sam Houston and his sixteen hundred and some odd soldiers was backed up by General Santa Anna and about six thousand of his little Mexican soldiers to a swamp called LaPointe. Now ole Santa Anna had left Reynosia, Mexico, about a year and a half before then, hell-bent on burning Texas ranches and settlements to the ground. Now, you boys remember this was 1836, and some of them ranches had some slaves. Goddammit, you boys listening?"

Yawn.

"Yes, sir."

"Now, on one of them ranches there was this high-yellow Negro girl named Emily West, and Santa Anna took her with him when he killed those poor souls what owned her. Anyhow, backed up to LaPointe with not much hope of surviving the day, Sam Houston sends my kinfolk up a tall pine tree at about the same time ole Santa Anna was taking that light-skinned girl into his tent for his 'siesta,' and I assume, some more ungentlemanly pursuits. When my great-great-granddaddy came down that tree and told Sam Houston what was going on, Sam ordered his men to prepare for battle. What they didn't kill ran like hell, and later on my great-great-granddaddy wrote a song about that girl, Emily West, and he called it 'The Yellow Rose of Texas.'"

I always allowed that Uncle Laurice brought Sammie here every summer just to get shed of him for three months, but Patty insisted that he brought him here to humble us and to show us that since we weren't born in the Great State somehow we were inferior. Maybe our craniums weren't as full or our penises weren't as long. Whatever the reason, his love for the Great State was as resolute as was Cro-Magnon man's resolve to outrun the saber-toothed tiger. I would have bet my last dollar that if Charles Darwin had been first cousin to Sammie, *The Origin of Species* would never have been written.

The most sadistic thing Patty ever did that I've witnessed was directed toward my cousin from Texas. Every time I think about it, my bottom side still remembers the terrible beating Patty and I got that night. Uncle Laurice couldn't bring him to Georgia that year. Instead, he sent him on the train with a shipping tag tied through a buttonhole in his shirt. Sammie had arrived for his annual summer visit wearing his brand-new, Red Camel, "gallused" overalls with the tag still sewn to the right hip pocket. Patty said that Shithead's daddy did it to show us inferior Georgians that being from Texas meant that you could have new overalls anytime of the year, instead of just the first week of school. The morning after Sammie's arrival, the three of us were getting dressed for the day, and Sam Houston couldn't find his clean underwear. Patty said, "Hell, boy, around here, we men don't wear underwear while we're breaking in new overalls, but I guess you folks from Texas aren't that tough." Sam Houston got this wild look in his eyes, and I guessed that at this point

Sammie would have walked through hell barefoot to prove that anyone from the Great State of Texas was far superior to anyone from Georgia.

Minus underwear he put on his never-washed, blue denim, Red Camel, gallused overalls. The Royal Crown Cola thermometer nailed to the feed barn read 94 degrees Fahrenheit that afternoon as we passed it going home. Sammie was walking as if someone had taken a generous portion of forty-grit sandpaper to his private parts. After supper that night, and much squirming and fretting by an obviously very uncomfortable Sam Houston, Patty announced, "Uncle Charlie, have you seen the kerosene and turpentine? I'm a little chafed, and I intend to get rid of it." Uncle Charlie looked at Patty as if he thought he had completely lost his mind, but told him where the turpentine and kerosene were.

Later, when Uncle Charlie had gone to bed and Patty had gone to the kitchen to "treat his chafe," Sammie asked me in a low voice if a mixture of kerosene and turpentine would really cure a raw bottom. And I, little Matty, for the first time since Patty and I were born, got to administer the coup de grace. I told him, "The way I do it, when I'm raw between my legs is, I mix up equal parts of turpentine and kerosene in a bowl and I splash it all over my private parts all at one time. It's going to sting a little bit though." Later that night, when all the dogs on the plantation had stopped barking and Sammie was down to a few jerking sobs, Uncle Charlie beat Patty and me to within an inch of our lives. Everywhere we went the next day the people on the plantation talked about the panther they heard screaming the night before.

CHAPTER 4

The Colonel

COLONEL O'HEARN WAS THE FINEST OLD GENTLEMAN I HAVE ever known. He lived his life by a code of honor that was completely undisputed by anyone who knew him. When he gave someone his word, the deed was as good as done. He was also at the vanguard of the proponents for a safe and unpolluted environment. He constantly voiced the need for husbandry of the land and its nonhuman inhabitants.

The Colonel was a prince among men. He was lean and muscular for his age and could outwalk any man on the plantation through the brush and bush in search of a game trail or quail roost. His hair was totally white and shone like fine silver threads in the sun as he made his way without benefit of a hat around the land daily. He exuded gentility in a fashion that didn't intimidate. He looked down on no man and admonished only those who violated civil law or civil reason. He considered ignorance and illiteracy to be a social malaise that could be eradicated if enough people cared. He was a Republican in a staunchly Democratic South but everyone forgave him for this. He was loved and respected by everyone on the plantation and no one wanted the bright blue eyes set in a finely chiseled face staring at them with an agitated expression in place. He was King Arthur in Camelot.

Each time the Colonel came to the plantation he brought Patty and me little gifts, and always books, and before he would leave us, he always admonished us to "be good stewards of the land, and keepers of its creatures. If you take one thing from the land, then replace it with as much or more than you took." Several times he told us the story of Tecumseh, the chief of the Shawnee. "The man was a man of nature, of peace and great understanding. He knew the earth rhythms as only a red man can. He told the white man two hundred years ago, 'You do not own the land, nor does any man. The earth is a living, breathing, thing. Treat it as such or it will be destroyed as are all living things.'" The Colonel practiced his admonishments to a fine degree and over the years contributed a fortune to nonprofit conservation organizations. He and Uncle

Charlie made a deal in which the Colonel supplied all the seed and fertilizer necessary to plant as many wild bird and animal feed plots as Uncle Charlie could muster from the surrounding land owners. In exchange, Uncle Charlie got carte blanche foxhunting rights to all the land the Colonel owned, and a good portion of the surrounding properties.

In the county where we lived some of the small cotton farmers and rural day laborers poached the larger plantation properties frequently and mercilessly. The poachers usually hit swiftly and were gone before they could be detected. They hunted the deer and rabbit late at night using spotlights mounted on their pickup trucks. When they killed, the game would be thrown on the back of the truck, and the poachers would quickly drive away. The plantation owners, particularly Colonel O'Hearn, despised this practice and made concerted efforts to control it. He constantly alerted the employees on the plantation that stopping the poachers was their most important job. He had Uncle Charlie, and Aunt Hattie's husband, Press, officially deputized by the local sheriff. They had arrest powers as did the full-time deputies. Press's sole job was to police the land. He had several verbal exchanges with trespassers, but he carried no gun because he figured that any show of force bred force.

Press was a powerful man, quiet and self-controlled. He was an excellent horseman, and the Colonel gave him a big black Morgan stallion that he rode as he kept a vigilant eye for poachers.

It may have seemed hypocritical for the Colonel to bring in guests to hunt for quail and be so adamantly opposed to the other hunters. He explained to us that we raised the birds just as a chicken farmer might raise his chickens and we harvested the birds for food. We always gave back more than we took, and we never wasted what we harvested.

The Colonel used the plantation mostly to entertain the people he did business with, but I knew if he didn't feel responsible for keeping a family conglomerate intact and out of the hands of incompetent relatives, he would have lived there full-time. When we were small children, he often told Patty and me that he could probably charge the people who hunted for free now and make more money than he was making on all the rest of his businesses. We would nod our heads in agreement. It never occurred to either of us to question anything he said. To us, the simple fact that he said it made it irrefutable.

There was no question in my mind that the Colonel was inordinately fond of Patty and me, and in a way, I suppose it set us apart from the other employees on the plantation. The difference was often so subtle that even the one perpetrating the partiality was usually unaware of it. For instance, when Patty and I were too young to do anything but simple menial tasks, like cleaning manure out of the stables or something less offensive such as walking to the main road to get the day's mail, if there were four boys to do the two different tasks, we always got the less offensive ones. We also got to ring the big cast-iron bell hailing the noon meal and quitting time. When the Colonel came to the plantation, for as long as I can remember, unless he was traveling with someone, his first stop was at our house at the crossroads. Always formal, and with emotion never penetrating his stoic facade, he somehow always managed to touch us in some small way. He would lift us off the porch when we were small, or something, anything, to make physical contact, without having to say, "I care for you." Always, too, it seemed that every time we needed anything: shoes, lunch boxes, shirts and jeans, sharp knives, or any other of the hundreds of things growing boys need, a package, wrapped in plain brown paper with no return address, would be delivered by the RFD mail carrier.

Through the years of our youth and on into our early teenage years, the Colonel continued the practice.

■　■　■

CHIEF AND NATE WERE ECHOWAH'S NUMBER-ONE HUNTING guides, both black and both about as big as live oak trees. They were both, also, probably the best bird dog guides in the South, if not the world. I believed they could really and truly carry on a conversation with a bird dog.

I never knew what Chief's real name was. One day, when I was small, I was at the main house visiting Aunt Hattie and she told me that Chief's great-grandfather had been a Zulu warrior and chief of his tribe, so from his first day on the plantation, everyone called him Chief. Chief was so attuned to the harmony and rhythm of the natural order of the earth that he required only a turning of pages in the book of nature to read things that the ordinary man didn't know existed, never even saw. The very winds whispered to him mysterious messages, and he foretold the fate of nature and the universe by the secret language of cloud linings and the circle around the moon, or through the messages of the woolyworm, cicada, and the tree frog. A sun dog at noon carried a different message from a sun dog at midafternoon. He knew these things, but he didn't know how he knew. I considered what little I gleaned from his vast knowledge of nature to be sacrosanct. When Chief was seen with fishing pole and bait can, everyone on the plantation not working headed for the bait bed. The fish would be biting that day.

Chief was distinctively different from anyone else I

ever knew. He never spoke first, but when spoken to, he was always flawlessly polite but to the point. He never squandered words. He was a kind and gentle man. I never heard him raise his voice, even on the two occasions I had personally seen him mad. Even then he was totally in control of himself and his emotions. He was also the only one on the plantation that was never, and I mean never, the victim of Patty's macabre sense of humor. Patty would never admit it, but he not only respected Chief, he was scared of him.

Chief was so in tune with nature that everyone relied on his uncanny judgment to tell them everything from when to plant their gardens, to when the white-tail deer would leave their bedding-down place and start to move. Uncle Charlie would always ask Chief when to stop strip-burning the woods for fear of burning up quail nests, and Chief would examine the blackberry bushes in late winter and tell him when the female quail would start nesting. I asked him how he knew by looking at a blackberry bush when quail were going to lay eggs. He told me, "Matty, those little birds are so dumb that they would starve to death when they are first hatched if something wasn't right there for them to eat. Now the good Lord put something in that grown bird's head that would make her hatch her young at exactly the same time as blackberries got ripe. Now all you got to do is know how long before the blackberries get ripe."

"Chief, how do you tell when the blackberries are going to be ripe?"

"Matty, ain't you got something to do besides ask questions?" he would ask with gentle impatience. I would get my feelings hurt, and he would say, "If I tell you how to tell when the blackberries are going to be ripe do you promise not to ask anything else today?" I think that Chief talked more with me than anyone else. It might have been because I asked him more questions than anyone else.

■ ■ ■

NATE WAS SIX FEET EIGHT INCHES TALL AND TALKED WITH A precise, clipped speech that I thought at the time was a French accent. The Colonel occasionally addressed Nate affectionately as "mon papillon fatale." When we were children, Uncle Charlie told Patty and me that the Colonel was calling Nate "my deadly butterfly." This puzzled me, so he explained that Nate had once been a soldier in the Senegalese army, part of a company assigned to the Colonel's command in North Africa during World War II. The German field marshal, Rommel, known as Desert Fox, was at the time in control of North Africa. The Allies' objective was to "cut off the serpent's head" by any means possible. The Colonel used the Senegalese company to undermine the morale of the Nazi soldiers assigned to the treeless desert expanse that dominated their station in North Africa. The Senegalese company represented the closest thing to cloning that anyone at the time had ever seen. Each man's height deviated but a few centimeters, if at all, from the whole. Each man's weight was within a few pounds of the average. The Senegal policy of isolationism, coupled with the dread others felt for them, was the basis for the sameness and purity of bloodlines.

When the European-based German soldiers first met a bagpipe-led Scottish brigade clad in their battle kilts, they laughed and called them the Ladies from Scotland. Before the battle was over, they called them the Bitches from Hell. When the North African–based German soldiers first encountered an army of six-foot-eight-inch, two-hundred-pound, khaki-clad men who looked as if they had been reproduced by a copying machine, the Germans didn't crack a smile. They took them seriously.

The Colonel used the uncanny night stealth of the Senegalese combatants to his advantage. He would send them into known enemy positions at night with their razor-sharp curved knives to kill whomever they could without making any noise whatsoever. I could imagine those Nazi bastards waking up from a sound sleep in hell with throats cut from ear to ear. I could also imagine Nate fully enjoying his task.

The Colonel and Nate seemed to share a bond that only fierce and mighty warriors share. After the war, the Colonel asked Nate to come to Georgia and work on the plantation.

■　■　■

Preston Leroy Angry was Aunt Hattie's husband. He had walked up to the back door of the plantation house in the spring of 1911 looking for work and food or preferably both. Aunt Hattie was a young woman working here at the time. She heard his knock and answered the door. She flushed and felt hot. He stammered and unbuttoned his top shirt button, and her chances of living a single life diminished greatly. The Colonel's daddy owned the plantation and was here at the time. Press approached him, his large hands wringing his old shapeless felt hat. He asked for a job. The Colonel's daddy asked Press where he was from and what he was called. The man replied, "People who know me call me Press, but my name is Preston Leroy Angry, and if you're looking for letters of references or an explanation of what I've been doing or where I've been, I don't have any, but if you're looking for a man who won't steal from you and who'll work hard for you, then I'm him." He lived up to his promises until the end.

He had been a soldier, a part of one of the black horse cavalry units in the United States army that was formed for frontier duty. The Indians had long since ceased to be a threat when the Mexican Civil War erupted in 1910, and his unit was sent to the Rio Grande to preserve its neutrality. A Mexican named Doroteo Arango had raged a campaign of lawlessness and violence since, at age sixteen, he had killed the man who raped his sister. And now he marshaled the largest army in Mexico. The world immortalized him as Pancho Villa, but Uncle Sam's only aim was to keep him out of Texas. Hate and strong drink led an abusive white sergeant to the black cavalry bivouac. When Press wouldn't lick the dust off the white sergeant's boots as instructed, two blows were exchanged. The first, from a riding crop, left a permanent scar from Press's ear to his chin. The second blow left the sergeant with a broken neck, trying unsuccessfully to keep his soul from leaving his body.

Press walked to Georgia, sleeping in daylight and walking at night, dodging the traffic of normal commerce on the main roads and skirting the populated areas when he came to them.

For Patty and me, he fit easily into the role of wise teacher of things that couldn't be learned elsewhere. Of all the people on the plantation who looked after us as children, next to the Colonel, I liked Press best. As I grew toward that magic age when you know everything, I often sought his soft-spoken wisdom, while Patty sought the more earthy advice rendered by Nate or Uncle Charlie.

CHAPTER 5

Saturday Night

FROM THE EARLIEST TIME I CAN REMEMBER AND COULD TELL Saturdays from any other day, Uncle Charlie would on that day take a bath and shave, whistling some nameless tune the whole time. He would dress up in his best clothes, start the Lincoln, and head for Albany. When we were too young to stay by ourselves, he always got Aunt Hattie to stay with us. Albany was thirty miles away, and my guess is that it had more beer joints and whorehouses than any town the same size in the entire United States.

Albany was also in the section of the Bible Belt that sang the Hallelujah chorus. The city was politically in the tight reins of hard-line men who had definite opinions of right and wrong. You could spend more time in jail for double-parking at the post office than for driving back-wards drunk and crashing through the front door of one of the local brothels.

Uncle Charlie always got back late on Saturday night, smelling of cheap whiskey and cheaper perfume and singing. You could hear him a quarter-mile away. "If the ocean was whiskey, and I was a duck, I'd dive to the bottom, and never come up. Whup—by God, I'll drink to that. This calls for an orgasm."

He usually stumbled over everything between his car and the front room, and every Saturday I waited up with Aunt Hattie just to listen to the lie he was going to tell her that night. He was a master. He'd say something like, "Aunt Hattie, I'm so sorry I'm late again, but I was in the A & P waiting my turn for my coffee to be ground, and this group of fair-haired, fair-skinned women surrounded me. They did something, God knows what, to render me unconscious, and when I awoke I was in a strange place with these women, and their leader spoke and said that they were a part of Hitler's experiment to produce a superior Aryan race of people, and that I had been chosen to be the sire of all their offspring. Aunt Hattie, they forced me to drink all this liquor, then they raped and ravaged my body. And only after a good deal of time had elapsed and they were all sexually exhausted was I able to slip away and come home. Now, I know that story is hard to believe, but you know for a fact that I would never drink this much liquor on my own, don't you?" Aunt Hattie would fuss and fume and warn him of the fate of breakers of the laws that Moses brought down from the heights of Sinai.

When I was small, I asked the Colonel if he had ever been to Paris. He said, "No, Matty, and I've always wanted to go, but I think I'd rather pay for your Uncle Charlie to go, then let him tell me about it."

When I told Uncle Charlie what the Colonel had said, he observed, "Well, I'll tell you, Matty. I never have been one to let the truth interfere with a good story. Any story worth telling is worthy of embellishment."

Patty and I talked for hours about Uncle Charlie's Saturdays, and inevitably, one of us would speculate on the possibility of his ever letting us go with him.

The day before the poachers burned the woods on the far side of the plantation to run rabbits out was mine and Patty's twelfth birthday. The wind had been coming from the northwest for two days. This was a dry wind, but typical for October, and the direction of the fire and smoke would drive the game toward the property line where a clay road divided the plantation land from the land of a farmer named Bunk Bartlet. The small farm had long since given up productivity to the constant practice of single cropping with cotton year after year.

Because of Nate's height, he looked thin and not very strong. I'm here to lay claim otherwise.

The morning of the fire Patty and I were helping Nate hitch a perfectly matched pair of big red mules to a hunting wagon. It was Saturday. The mules looked like mirror images, each with a white blaze on his forehead and four white stockings. The Colonel had just recently bought them as fully broken, but they were still a little green. When Nate walked behind the mules to hitch the harness to the singletree on the wagon, one of them kicked him on the shin and knocked the "mon Dieu, mon Dieu, mon Dieu" out of him. He hopped around on one leg holding his hurt leg for a while. Then he lay on the ground, rolling from side to side, holding his mule-kicked shin.

I would have been okay if I hadn't heard Patty make a sound like a dying goat. I burst into a fit of giggling similar to one suffered during one of the rare times Patty and I had gone to church at Macedonia, and a small white dog had marched through the open doors and hiked his leg on the pew in front of us. I decided that the best place to giggle uncontrollably was about two hundred feet from where Nate lay groaning. Nate finally got off the ground, and taking great strides while always favoring his gimpy right leg, he circled that mule and wagon rig three times, tightening the circle each time. When he made the third circumference, he stopped in front of the guilty mule and said in French something that I presumed to be "Are you going to kick me ever again?" The mule just stood there and Nate hit that mule between the eyes with his bare fist, and I quit giggling. The mule hit the ground as cold as turkey on the Saturday after Thanksgiving. Nate then stepped over in front of the other mule and asked this mule the same question (and again I'm assuming) in French and I hope lightning strikes me if that damn mule didn't shake his head from side to side.

Patty had decided to giggle close to where I was. He cupped his hands and yelled, "Nate, if you killed that mule the Colonel's going to kill your ass." Nate started limping toward us, so we decided to go see what Chief was doing. We outran Nate easily.

"One of these days Nate is going to beat you to a pulp," I said. "From now on will you not make him mad when I'm around. He might beat me up too."

"Do you think I'm a fool? If you'll notice, you'll see I don't ever provoke him unless I can outrun him."

Nate stopped and looked west. "Go get your uncle," he yelled. I looked in the direction Nate's eyes were glued, his gimpy leg forgotten, and saw the smoke. This was one month before the opening of quail season, and fire meant no birds would inhabit the burned-over areas and the Colonel would be wanting to know why this had happened. Before Patty or I could reach the main house to ring the bell, Nate had caught up with us, and before the first ring of the dinner bell had quit resounding through the quietness, Press and Uncle Charlie were on their way to the place where we waited.

The pickup truck sped over the clay road that led toward the fire. Me, Patty, and Nate, were on the back. Uncle Charlie and Press were in the front. Chief was on his way through the fire breaks on a tractor with a small fire plow attached. We had gotten shovels and axes to cut brushy-topped bushes to use to beat the fire out. The plan was to beat the fire out toward the interior of the plantation and try to hold it until Chief could get there and plow a break around the fire. What we saw when we rounded the curve before we got to the fire was not what anyone had expected.

Bunk Bartlet and eight or ten dirty men, all with shotguns, stood in the road with guns ready. If a rabbit succeeded in making it through the smoke, avoiding the fire, and made it to the road the blast of a shotgun would end the unsuspecting animal's life. A growing pile of dead rabbits was scattered around a half-empty gallon jug of moonshine whiskey.

The truck stopped fifty feet shy of the first man, and Uncle Charlie stepped from the truck. Press and Nate joined him. "You boys enjoying yourselves?" Uncle Charlie spoke.

"It ain't none of your business, Charlie," Bunk answered. "We is on a public road, and when them rabbits hit the public road they belong to all o' us."

"The rabbits are coming from the plantation because one of you set the fire."

"Don't know what you're talking about, Charlie. Seems to me you could be taking all this a little too seriously." He looked around to the nods of his buddies and turned back to Uncle Charlie. "You might best get y'all's asses on back where you came from." He grinned, and black shadows of rotting teeth made his teeth look jagged and sharp like I imagined a vampire's to be.

Patty and I joined the other three. We found ourselves facing the cold stares of defiant men whose emotions had been fueled by white whiskey and Bunk Bartlet. I heard the groan of the tractor Chief was driving as it plowed the perimeters of the fire. Everything seemed to move in slow motion as I watched the drama unfold. Uncle Charlie told them, "I'm going to arrest you for shooting in a public road then. You boys put down your guns and come with me."

Almost as a unit the men picked up the dead rabbits and whiskey and stepped across the ditch to the land owned by Bunk. "Now I'm on my land, Charlie. You or any of your crowd set foot on my land and I'll blow you to hell for trespassing."

I saw Patty square his shoulders and start to walk toward the spot where Bunk stood. I reached for him and missed so I didn't have any choice but to follow. I couldn't let him get killed by himself. My heart felt like it was running away. Patty walked directly in front of Bunk and stared into the ugly face and squinting eyes. "When the Colonel gets here he's going to kill your ass graveyard-dead, Bunk." He turned to leave, then turned back and kicked Bunk as hard as he could on his kneecap. Bunk's mouth dropped open first, then he dropped his shotgun and grabbed his knee and sat down hard on the ground. I don't know why, but I picked up the shotgun. Patty calmly walked back to our truck, and I followed closely. Uncle Charlie took the gun from my hands and stuck the barrel between the bumper hangers on the truck. He bent the barrel ninety degrees and threw it across the ditch. We drove slowly home after the fire had been contained. Nobody talked. Wasn't any need to.

Three weeks later Patty and I were promoted to the position of assistant hunting guides to help when Nate or Chief needed us. I guess the men figured we had earned the position. I didn't tell anyone how I wet my pants a little.

CHAPTER 6

Raw Oysters

THE FIRST TIME I EVER SAW CHIEF REALLY MAD WAS THE week after we got promoted. Patty was asking Chief and Nate which one had the best bird dog, and as was his standard MO he wouldn't let it rest until he had provoked a friendly disagreement.

"I should have known y'all would get in an argument," he told them. "I figure the only way to settle this is to have a hunt-off."

"What is this hunt-off?" Nate asked.

"A hunt-off is kind of like a fuck-off. Very few differences in fact. Both are used to break a tie. The only difference is that a hunt-off breaks a tie between two hunting dogs, and a fuck-off is what the judges do to break a tie in a French beauty contest."

It was decided, by drawing the longest straw, which one was to get me and which one Patty as sworn eyewitnesses and scorekeepers. We decided the hunting courses, and limited the hunt from 8:00 A.M. until noon the following Sunday morning. The rules were that the first dog to point, each time a bird was found, would get three points. If the other dog backed or honored the point, he would get one point. If a dog failed to back the other dog's good point, he would get one point taken from his score. And a dog that gave a false point would get two points taken away.

I don't know how Nate did it without waking every dog Chief had and consequently waking Chief. No man this side of Senegal other than Nate that could have sneaked into Chief's dog pens that Saturday night and poured red pepper all over his dogs. The next morning the big liver pointer Chief had chosen for the match couldn't have smelled its own rear end. After the score was twenty-one, Nate, to minus seven, Chief, the big black man called his dog and started looking him over from the inside of his nostrils to the tip of his tail. Every few seconds while he was doing this, he would sort of glance up at Nate. After he had thoroughly examined the big pointer, he slowly stood up, six feet six inches. Slowly and deliberately he took his coat off, folded it up, and laid it on the ground. I had never seen Chief when he didn't have on a loose-fitting, white, homemade cotton shirt, so when he took off his shirt and I saw what to me looked like two Joe Louises packed into one body, I told Patty, "I think it's time for you and me to go see if Uncle Charlie needs any help fixing lunch."

Patty said, "Let's stay here and watch Nate get his ass beat."

"Patty, sooner or later one of them is going to realize that all this is your fault. You stay here if you want to."

Uncle Charlie looked at us suspiciously when we came home early, and I asked if he needed any help.

Nate evidently stayed several rounds, then took the count to a full ten that day. He looked awful. We saw him late that afternoon and Patty said, "Nate, I sure do hope you got the tag number of that Mack truck that ran over you, and I sure am proud them tigers didn't eat you when they got through clawing you up, and I'm mighty happy you didn't get your brains knocked out when them wild horses drug your ass all over this plantation. Matty, I was sure wrong this morning when I told you that Chief was going to beat Nate's ass. I don't believe he even touched his butt, but he sure did a fine job of beating on his head."

At 63,450 feet above sea level, the atmospheric pressure gets so thin that blood will boil at exactly the temperature of a person's body, which is 98.6 degrees Fahrenheit. I told Patty he'd better shut up because I figured Nate was approaching that altitude. So we left to see if Uncle Charlie needed any help fixing supper. There isn't a doubt in my mind that Nate would have caught us that day if both his legs hadn't been gimpy.

Three days passed before we got the nerve to find Nate. We were walking from our house to the big house and saw him sitting on the wooden fence by the stables. We were about to cut across behind the dog pens and avoid him when we saw the Colonel and Press ride out of the woods and across the hay field toward the stables. "Let's go, Matty. The son of a bitch can't kill us if the Colonel's there."

The Colonel and Press got there at the same time as Patty and I. He and Press spoke their greetings. Nate glared at us then looked up and said, "Morning, Colonel, Press. Did anyone step in dog dung? I smell something."

The Colonel looked at Nate and said, "Did a truck hit you, Nate?" I bit my lip until it bled. Patty walked over to the horse trough and splashed water on his face. Press's big horse pranced nervously.

"No, Colonel. Something worse."

The Colonel didn't pry. He told us, "I heard several shots last night, and Press and I have been riding since dawn. We found the carcasses of two deer. Only the hindquarters and back strap were gone. This must be stopped. If any of you hear a shot at night, try to locate the vehicle the poachers are in and get the tag number. Do not confront them." He looked at me and his features softened. "I'm proud of you and Patty for standing up to those men." He turned to Nate and said, "Nate, when these young men aren't busy helping you and Chief, I want you to teach them about the skeet range. I'll tell Charlie to give them a raise also." Nate fumed.

The next to last step up the employment ladder on the plantation was backup, or assistant, hunting guide. We had made it to that position by being stupid. The number-one, boss position was full-time, do-nothing-else, kiss-nobody's-ass, get-what-you-want-when-you-want-it, hunting guide. Echowah Plantation had two senior hunting guides, Nate and Chief. When you worked your way up the ladder to the rear of their ranks with any aspiration toward advancement, the wall between you and them made the Berlin Wall look like a split-rail fence.

■ ■ ■

RURAL SCHOOLS IN THE SOUTH IN THE FIFTIES ALLOWED students to be absent from school thirty-one days each year so that farm children could help with the harvest. Patty and I took every day allowable that year starting in mid-October until the last day of hunting season. We helped with the hunting parties and did anything else we possibly could to earn money. My favorite thing was riding on the hunting wagons with Chief or Nate when they took a party out. Patty would usually start the day riding the wagon with me and Chief or Nate, but it was indeed a rarity when they didn't send him home walking before the day was over. The plain truth was his big mouth was usually the culprit that made a long-distance pedestrian out of Patty.

A hunting guide's job consisted of taking three trained bird dogs and driving a matched pair of mules hitched to a hunting wagon with a typical hunting party of four people on board. We ordinarily hunted with two dogs on the ground and a reserve one in the dog box. When the dogs pointed the guide stopped the wagon; and the hunters fanned out and walked toward the covey until it flushed.

As assistant hunting guides that year we occasionally filled in for or assisted Nate and Chief. During the regular hunting season we normally had two four-person hunting parties as guests on the plantation. One party was guided by Chief, and one by Nate. When there were too many amateur shooters for a normal two-hunting-party retinue, Nate and Chief separated the two parties into three or four smaller ones. They always gave Patty and me the more experienced hunters. This vastly decreased the probability of anyone getting shot, or nearly shot, or of anyone soiling his pants. When you're hunting quail with a normal contingency of four experienced, or inexperienced but rational, hunters, and the dogs point and the covey breaks cover, the hunters have usually positioned themselves far enough apart to eliminate any risk of being in another hunter's line of fire. On the other hand, when you have four novice hunters in one party, each armed with a lethal weapon and each with an inordinate amount of adrenaline coursing through his veins, and a covey of twelve excited quail burst cover, frequently the quail are the safest things around.

Often that fall when I rode the hunting wagon with Nate and the hunting party posed any danger to him, real or imagined, he would make the announcement when the dogs pointed a covey, "Please, no one get off the wagon until I remove it from the position it is in. When I tell you, walk in the direction the dogs are pointing. Matty and I will remain with the wagon to better observe the shooting." As soon as they started walking toward the dogs, Nate and I would stand on the opposite side of the wagon until the shooting stopped. Once someone shot the side of the wagon and the mules ran, leaving Nate and me exposed. Nate held his hands high over his head like I had seen the outlaws do on the television at the big house. I held my hands up too.

Patty and I were taking our first party out by ourselves several weeks after we had been promoted.

Hunting courses were laid out so that at approximately noon, all the hunting parties would convene at a pavilion-type building in a pretty little meadow. The staff from the kitchen at the main house would be waiting there with sandwiches, or cold fried quail, or whatever the Colonel wanted for that day's noon meal. This particular day, as it happened, the head cook from our house had gone into town earlier and the Central of Georgia overnighter from Appalachicola, Florida, had left several bushels of fresh, select oysters for one of the other plantations at the train station. Our cook had talked their cook out of two bushels of them. Lunchtime came, and Chief, Nate, Patty and I, and sixteen guests arrived at the lunch pavilion to a sight that was familiar to the guests but absolutely alien to me and the other three subsophisticates.

We gawked open-mouthed as the guests started actually eating these nasty-looking little things whole. They would take a toothpick, get the oyster out of its shell, put it on a soda cracker, pop the whole thing in their mouths, and talk about how good it was.

The four of us sat in the far corner watching. Patty asked. "What in the hell are they eating?" Nobody answered. He waited a minute and asked, "Chief, do you know?"

"Oysters."

"Would you mind elaborating? I don't know any more now than I did before you made that long speech. Why don't you ever talk anyway?"

"I was raised to talk only when what I had to say had some importance. It would be a far more pleasant world if you would do the same."

Patty got up and walked over and talked to Doris Lee, who was serving the meal. He came back and sat down. "An oyster is a saltwater shellfish kin to the creek mussels around here. You're supposed to eat them raw." He looked triumphantly at Chief.

We ate our sandwiches in silence but I could tell that it was getting the best of Patty. He announced, "By God, I'm going to try one of those little sons of bitches. Try one with me, Nate."

"I'm not eating anything that looks like the by-product of a chicken with diarrhea."

"Chief, can I bring you back one?"

Chief had pushed his empty paper plate to the center of the table. "Had enough."

Patty tried one; then he tried another. Then he put two on crackers and handed me one and ate the other. I told him, "I'm not eating this thing, the guts are still in it."

"If you don't eat it I'm going to tell everybody what you

were doing the other day when I caught you looking at one of Uncle Charlie's girlie magazines and you thought nobody was at home."

Mine stayed down, and fifteen minutes and uncountable "I-double-dog-dare-yous" later, Nate agreed to eat one, under the condition that he be allowed to eat all the soda crackers he wanted to first. The soda crackers obviously dried Nate's throat. When he tried to swallow one of Appalachicola's finest selects, it made it to his Adam's apple and wouldn't go any further. I saw Nate's eyes start to bulge and his chest started to convulse, and the blood vessels in his temples swelled and pulsated with each heartbeat. With a mighty cough Nate dislodged the oyster from his throat. Apparently, it went up his nasal passage and halfway out his left nostril and lodged again. Nate grappled with the thing trying to pull it out, but it was too slick to hold onto, so he put his thumb over his right nostril and, with all the wind he had left, he blew the slimy thing out, and it hit the floor and splattered.

Sixteen horrified captains of commerce put down what they were eating and quietly filed out of the building. Some gagged. Patty and I ran for the woods where we laughed until I got choked and threw up. When we started back to the house, not looking at each other to keep from laughing, Nate intercepted us. He leaned down and got uncomfortably close in my face and then he got real close in Patty's face, and in a voice that would have given a mass murderer chills, said, "If I ever hear the word *oyster* from either one of you little sons of bitches, you're going to be trying to explain to Satan what you're doing in hell at such a young age."

CHAPTER 7

Leighanne

ALL AT ONCE, IT SEEMED WITHOUT ANY FOREWARNING, I turned thirteen and my body went crazy. Fine black hair appeared on my lip and chin. I grew tall and I woke up nights and had feelings in my lower body parts that were strange. I wanted to be an adult, but I wanted to know more of youth. I still wanted to chase butterflies and rainbows.

Uncle Charlie came in our room one morning to wake us up and saw my obvious predicament. "Looks like your writing instrument is getting some lead in it."

"Sir?" I said, trying to hide the thing that was elevating the covers.

"Looks like your pencil's getting some lead in it. Don't tell me you haven't tried to pee your name in the dirt with that thing."

"No sir," I lied.

"I have. Let a few women write with it too. Still would be, if my neighbor up in Tennessee hadn't recognized his wife's handwriting."

My first love, and my first sexual experience, were with the most stunningly beautiful fifteen-year-old girl ever created. Her name was Leighanne Carter. She was eighteen months older than I, and she looked like the Lord had spent a good deal of overtime creating a being most perfect. Then man exerted his influence, it seems, more gently, and somehow improved on the perfect. I believe God was just showing off the day he created her. She, to me, was the dancer's leap, or the actor's passion, or the artist's vision. Each move she made was grace, each word she spoke was poetry, her laughter was the tinkling of bells that vibrated in my mind and overflowed to my soul. Her frown was the sounding of cymbals. She would look at me and a smile would play at the corners of her mouth and my legs would automatically be rendered into useless rubber with knots tied for knees and ankles. The need to indulge in sexual fantasies was ever-present in my young life, and Leighanne filled these needs my every waking moment.

Leighanne lived almost in the middle of our school bus route and about five miles from our house. We lived at a crossroads north of a small town called Notchaway, which was geographically in the center of Chickasaw County and should have been the county seat by virtue of its location but wasn't.

The school bus came near our house twice, once near the beginning of its route and again toward the end.

The moment I decided I was in love with Leighanne and decided to make her my love slave and to move to the Amazon and establish a rubber plantation and found an industrial empire and finally become benevolent benefactor and supreme ruler and commander-in-chief of South America, I started catching the bus for the long ride in the mornings and staying on the bus for the long ride in the afternoons so that I could ride longer with her.

The driver, Mr. Calhoun, fussed about having to stop for me in the mornings, then having to stop a second time for Patty, but I think he understood my reason and his scolding at best was half-hearted. "Matty, why in the name of common sense do you want to ride this far every day?"

"Mr. Calhoun, if you had a brother like Patty, wouldn't you ride just to get away from him for a while?"

"Enough said."

My brother thought I was crazy. "Why the hell do you want to ride that dusty old rattletrap bus when you don't have to? Hell, Matty, you don't even like school, and people are beginning to say that I have a mentally retarded brother. Not that it bothers me, I've accepted the fact for years that when the brains were divided between you and me, you were slighted."

Uncle Charlie thought I was doing it to get out of afternoon chores. I would simply look down my nose at both of them and think about how much I was going to enjoy sending my army someday to arrest them and to take their stupid asses out to the middle of the goddam Amazon River and feed them to the piranha.

I was first on the bus every morning and always sat in the front seat behind Mr. Calhoun as he drove the bus. Sitting here allowed three things. It put me in a position where Mr. Calhoun knew that I wasn't misbehaving and therefore he wouldn't be focusing his rearview mirror on my position. I could turn around and look at any time. It allowed me the advantage of being occasionally lucky enough to look around at precisely the exact moment Leighanne Carter would cross her perfect legs and I would catch a fleeting glimpse of frilly lace and imagine all the tantalizing things a young boy who had recently gone from soprano to baritone can imagine. And it allowed me to be the first one off the sixty-passenger, 1952 model, Bluebird Student Supreme school bus, holding a Blue Horse writing tablet that hid an erection old men would kill for.

She had moved to Chickasaw County when I was twelve, and I think I loved her the moment I saw her. She was the only daughter of a hardscrabble sharecropper named Eli Carter and his once handsome wife whose features hard times had etched deeply. Mr. Carter farmed on halves, Alabama style, with whomever he traded with for the year. He chased the elusive dream of owning his own farm until the year they moved here to claim the farm his late bachelor uncle had bequeathed him.

I remember it was almost Christmas and I had been watching for the mail carrier to come from the south road. I saw dust, then jumped from the porch and ran to the mailbox to wait until the dust cloud would produce the dried mud-splattered sedan of the RFD carrier. It wasn't the mail carrier. The treasures and necessities of fifteen years of a hard life were haphazardly amassed and tied down with grass rope on the back of an army surplus truck. Mr. Carter shared the front seat with the more precious possessions obviously inherited from dead relatives.

When the truck stopped at the crossroads, a big sedan followed and obediently rocked on worn-out shock absorbers and waited for the stifling red dust to settle about it. I saw her on the passenger side. Hair the color of summer wheat caressed the most beautiful face I'd ever seen. Deep blue intelligent eyes stared back at me as I watched the two vehicles leave the intersection and resume their journey to the farm Mr. Carter now owned.

She watched, turning her head to study me as the car gathered speed. I leaned heavily on the mailbox trying to look different, more debonair, than how I imagined myself to look. The rotted post broke. I looked into her eyes as she passed and I fell to earth with the humiliating post. She smiled but did not laugh at my clumsiness, and I fell into the most absolute love a boy or man can experience.

No one could begin to imagine the sensations I felt that morning several months later. It was 7:32 A.M. Eastern Standard Time, October 10, 1957. A cool breeze was blowing; the dog fennel and yellow coneflower were in full bloom. The goldenrod flaunted its most brilliant mustard color. Leighanne Carter got her perfect body, mind, soul, and self on the bus and sat down in the seat next to me. An Egyptian mummy could breathe better than I could. When she spoke, my face felt as if it were on fire, and I had this overwhelming desire to run or urinate. I thought, "My God, I'm going to faint and wake up dead and in heaven."

She said, "Matty, I have cheerleading practice tonight, and I told my mother that I was going to ask you if maybe you could ride with me and maybe stay for the practice, in case I have a flat tire, since I don't really know how to fix a flat tire."

Instant amnesia struck. I knew she was talking to me, but I couldn't for the life of me remember my name.

Whoever I was finally answered in a voice that I didn't recognize, "I'd be honored to change your flat tire, and if you don't have a flat tire I'd be honored to make it go flat and then fix it." Sometimes I wished that Patty had been an only child.

She walked back to her regular seat and sat down, and this time I saw the lacy edges of black panties and realized after it was too late that I didn't have any books with me to conceal the obvious problem that had developed.

That afternoon after school, I tore my brother's clothes chest apart looking for a package of Sheik prophylactics he had bought the past summer to impress Shithead. When I found them, the cellophane had been torn off, and the package looked as if, on more than one occasion, it had seen the working parts of a Maytag. I stole them anyway, just in case, just in case, just in case. . . . The next hour, behind locked doors, I spent in front of a mirror practicing kissing, just in case. I kissed the back of my hand, the bedpost, the *Saturday Evening Post*, and anything else that cared to part its torrid, quivering lips and place them wetly on mine. I had read in one of the books Uncle Charlie kept under his mattress that the first time a girl has intercourse, she is "insufficiently lubricated to allow penetration; therefore a lubricant such as Vaseline should be generously applied to the male organ." I looked everywhere in the house for a jar of Vaseline Petroleum

Jelly and the closest thing I could find was Vicks VapoRub. I decided, in my dimwitted state, that this would do just as well or better than Vaseline. My body still flushes to this day when I think about that night.

From the time I perfected my kissing that afternoon until Leighanne got to my house, I was in a semicoma. The days were still long and reluctant to give up the heat of summer. I lay across my small bed and stared blankly at the half-opened window and watched the lacy curtains: hand-me-downs from the big house that Aunt Hattie had hung, waving gently with the sparse breeze. The faint aroma emanating from a late-blooming honeysuckle vine drifted through the open window and cast its magic, creating fantasies in my mind of exotic places, each occupied by Leighanne, each filled with wild love scenes.

Each half minute or so I would tear my eyes away from the hypnotic trance of the hula dancers disguised as curtains and search the room for the old Big Ben wind-up clock with the brass alarm ringers on top. Occasionally I would stagger up to check if the clock had stopped, even though the loud ticking could be clearly heard where I lay.

When she finally got there, after what seemed like the life span of small mammals, and blew the horn, something inside me, as old as life and as young as youth, zigzagged from my lower spine to the back of my neck and left goose bumps and little hairs standing at attention. My subliminal mind, a chromosome on my genes, something, had recognized the mating call even though my conscious mind didn't fully understand why I was doing certain things. Like a wild yearling wolf that had thrown his howl toward the moon and had heard a distant female answer, my soul had heard the answer to its howl.

Somehow I made it down the front porch steps without falling on my face. I walked rigidly to her car, trying to look casual and controlled. Immediately the meister of idiocy, whom I didn't recognize but knew must have been me, blurted, "Leighanne, I just want you to know that I love you and I want you to go to South America with me and I think you're the most beautiful girl in the whole world."

She was nervous too. She ran her tongue over her red lips and smiled, "Matty, do you really think I'm pretty?"

I managed to say, "I read something in school written by Christopher Marlowe about Helen of Troy. He said that her face was the face that had launched a thousand ships. Your face could launch the entire United States Navy." She blushed, but smiled.

When cheerleading practice was a few minutes old, Leighanne told Miss Suggs, the spinster teacher who had volunteered to coach the cheerleading team, that she had cramps and needed to go.

We left, she, nervous; me, pee-down-your-britches-leg excited, and she drove her father's big car straight to Macedonia Free Will Baptist Church. Macedonia was a small white clapboard church, nestled among moss-draped oaks and set several hundred feet back from the main road, as most country churches were back then. The yards were hard-packed sand, swept clean every Saturday by stern and unsmiling deacons' wives, and completely free of grass. Grassfree yards were commonplace, to prevent unattended woods fires from reaching the buildings.

Every country church had a cemetery on the back side, carefully laid out so that it wouldn't be in the direct line of sight of Sunday morning worshipers. But by turning their heads far enough, the not-so-righteous could see and contemplate their ultimate fate, and hopefully see the light of repentance. The headstones at Macedonia cemetery dated back to the early 1800s when the region was untamed. Many of the residents of the cemetery rested here as a result of losing altercations involving guns or knives, or spears and arrows.

Neither of us spoke until she switched the engine off. She turned toward me and softly said, "Matty, every single morning I get on that school bus, I go back to the fifth row and sit next to my best friend Cindy, and every single morning you turn your head exactly at the very moment I sit down and cross my legs. Now, I know that you've been trying to look up my dress for forever, and if you ever tell anyone, I swear to God I'll put rat poison in your lunch, but if you want to see me, then I don't think that you should try to sneak around and look, when all you have to do is ask."

I asked, and my soprano voice was gone forever. My moonlit howl was answered.

I generously applied the Vicks VapoRub to my male organ and tried to pull a dried-out, machine-washed, Sheik prophylactic over the Vicks and my penis. The first rubber shredded and then the other one burst and a high-pitched "Leighanne, I can't do it. The goddam rubber busted!" came out.

Then a slightly agitated, "Matty, will you calm down? I sneaked some out of my daddy's sock drawer."

I applied more Vicks.

I have noticed that when a person is terribly excited, he doesn't seem to notice pain. Later that night, I sat in a washtub half full of cold water, trying to abate the burning sensation on my genitalia, and for the next several days I walked around as if I were trying to balance a martini on my buttocks. Vicks VapoRub makes no allowance for stupidity: it will definitely take the skin off the penis of a thirteen-year-old boy.

CHAPTER 8

Keeping Secrets

THE NEXT DAY UNCLE CHARLIE ASKED ME, "WHY ARE YOU walking around like that, Matty? You constipated or something?"

"No sir, I guess I got red bugs on my privates."

"I got the red bugs once when I got the green-apple quickstep while I was foxhunting and had to make do with some Spanish moss. I'm here to tell you, don't ever substitute toilet paper with Spanish moss. My tallywacker swelled up about twice the normal size. I was glad when the itching finally stopped, but I kind of wish the swelling would have stayed. Should have took some pictures."

The next morning was Saturday, and Uncle Charlie asked if we'd like to go to town with him. We were almost fourteen years old, and Leighanne was gone for the weekend, so there wasn't any chance of seeing her. "You gents are getting on up in age and I was thinking, if you could get out of your chores this afternoon, y'all might enjoy going to one of them movie houses while I do my running around."

Two seconds later I was getting up off the floor after Patty accidentally ran over me trying to get to our room to change clothes. It occurred to me that we had never been to a movie in our lives, and we wouldn't know what to do, so I asked Uncle Charlie. "Uncle Charlie, I don't want Patty to make a fool out of himself when we get there. Can you tell me what we're supposed to do?"

"Well, to tell the truth, I never have been but to a few myself. As I recollect though, you go up to this little glassed-in closet outside the picture show, and there's most likely going to be a pretty girl in there. Give her your fifteen cents and she'll give each of you a little purple ticket to take to the front door." He paused and pushed his mustache back with his finger, one side then the other.

"What do we do when we get to the front door?"

"Well, let me think. Yep, right outside, a man, dressed up like the man who's in the advertisements for Philip Morris cigarettes. The one in that funny-looking round hat and suit with the stripes on the legs. He'll take your tickets, tear them in half, and give half of it back to you."

"What do we do then?"

"Goddammit, Matty, can't you figure nothing out? You go inside and stand around and do what everybody else is doing."

"What if everybody else is buying chocolate ice cream and something to drink and we ain't got no money?"

Uncle Charlie, freshly bathed and shaved with Old Spice on his face and Vitalis in his hair, which he combed straight back like Clark Gable's, cranked the Lincoln and we were off, pee-in-your-pants excited, to Albany.

He let us out at the theater with exact instructions. "You boys watch the thing they call . . . , I believe they call it a main feature. Anyway, watch it three times, then come out and I'll be waiting for you."

"What's a main feature, Uncle Charlie?"

"Patty, tell your thick-headed brother what a main feature is."

"It appears to me that there's three of us in this car that don't know what a main feature is," Patty answered, looking hard at Uncle Charlie.

We went to the ticket booth, which was exactly where Uncle Charlie said it would be—I, with a certain air of undisguised arrogance, because I knew something that Patty didn't. I explained to him, "This little glass closet is where we have to buy our purple tickets, which cost fifteen cents."

"What do we do then?"

"We have to take the tickets to that dressed-up man in the funny-looking round cap at the front door. We have to show our tickets to him so he'll let us in." It never occurred to me to tell Patty that the doorman would tear them in half to prevent them from being used again.

Patty was first to the door, and when Philip Morris tore his ticket in half, Patty's face turned beet red and he screamed at Philip Morris, "Goddam your soul to hell! You tore my ticket up and you're gonna buy me another one, or me and my brother are gonna beat hell out of you."

I walked over to the nearest wall and pretended to study the movie poster, shrouded behind glass, as the startled usher went to the ticket window and purchased a new ticket for Patty with his own money.

Three times we watched Lash Larue beat up every man in the saloon, kill every Indian north of the Pecos River, and rescue the prettiest woman I had ever seen, with the exception of Leighanne.

When we came out of the movie, it was dark, but the Lincoln was parked across the street, and Uncle Charlie was in the back seat drunk, asleep, snoring, and smelling like cheap perfume. We tried to wake him, but he muttered, "Leave me alone. Can't you see that I'm dead?"

"Uncle Charlie, please wake up. We need to go home, and me and Patty don't know how to drive."

Snorting and slurring his words he answered, "I don't know who you are but if you wake me up one more time, there's going to be a serious altercation involving pistols. Now leave me alone. I'm dead."

When we got home that night, I told Patty I thought he had done a pretty good job, never to have driven before, and he said he thought I had done pretty good, too, other than that line of parking meters I knocked down.

At breakfast the next morning Uncle Charlie looked awful. He fixed oatmeal for us, but couldn't eat himself, so he sat at the table trying to pick from us what had happened the night before. "Er, did you fellas enjoy the picture show?"

"It was pretty good. Matty acted the fool though."

"What did he do this time?"

"Well, this cowboy named Lash Larue was riding through a narrow gully and two Indians were on the top of the ledge and when Lash Larue went by they were going to shoot him. Matty yelled as loud as he could, 'Look out behind you.' I started to get up and move. I did get up and move when he did it the third time we saw the show."

"Er, I don't quite remember the drive home. Course now I was awfully tired and at my age you don't remember as good as when you're rested. Everything was all right, wasn't it?"

"Yes sir. You've got some new dents in your front bumper though."

I cringed because I knew Patty was going to tell.

"I'd be obliged if one of you shook my memory tree and caused me to remember how I did that."

Before Patty could answer I blurted, "Don't you remember, Uncle Charlie? You got something in your eye and you hit about ten parking meters in Albany."

"Those damned things are a nuisance to mankind anyway. Pretty soon them damned lawyers we send to the statehouse in Atlanta will be thinking of how they can charge people to fish or hunt or breathe the air for that matter."

■　■　■

OVER THE SPAN OF SEVERAL INCREDIBLY HAPPY MONTHS, Leighanne and I did everything contained in the repertoire of lovemaking positions listed in Uncle Charlie's books. We did a whole lot of things that weren't even in the books under Uncle Charlie's mattress. On warm spring days whenever I would sneak away from chores, she met me in a little grassy meadow next to the lake not quite a mile from the main house. The lake was called Lake Echo, for the nymph who loved Narcissus, but on more than one occasion when we were there, I yelled, "Leighanne, I love you!" And I never once heard an echo, from the lake or from her. We would spend hours doing absolutely nothing, or she would read to me. Sometimes she recited poems I had written for her or poems she had read. I found tiny wildflowers for her. I called her my meadow princess. In the spring I wove her tiaras of forsythia, and in late summer, I wove them of honeysuckle.

"Matty, why do you think that I love you? I've never told you how I feel." Wide blue eyes staring from the most beautiful face I'd ever seen watched for my reaction as she asked.

"Hope springs eternal in the human heart."

"No, seriously," she asked softly.

"Because, if you searched the universe, you would never find anyone who would love you more than I, and some of those feelings must have found a way inside you."

"Matty, can't you see that I simply can't allow myself to love you?"

"Then I can't allow myself to believe you. You are my reason for being."

"What if I told you that I didn't love you? Which is God's honest truth."

"Leighanne, when you talk, or laugh, or make any sound at all I hear music in me. It's hard to explain, but that's the song my soul hears because all I need to do is lie still at night and think of you and I hear the music again.

I don't believe that you don't love me. I think that you do. I think your soul sings to mine."

Sometimes she convinced me my love was unrequited. Most of the time, however, I knew without doubt that she was only afraid to admit she loved me. Like a perfect rose, she grew in all the right places, and blossomed and got more beautiful in all the right places, and got perfectly warm in the right places. I could swear that each time I saw her she was, by far, more beautiful than the time before.

On soggy, drizzly days, not fit for man nor beast, when the red-tailed hawk would sit on high bare limbs with its neck scrunched as far down as possible, looking miserable, because he knew that normal commerce would cease and the drizzle would ensure an empty stomach that night, we met at one of the little one-room cabins built for hunters to rest in or get out of the rain. We would lie on the cot holding each other as closely as possible to stay warm, or she sat with my head in her lap. She stroked my face and sang to me, or read a poem I had written, and I silently asked God to not let it end. On some days we walked holding hands through the woods, and we'd talk about our dreams and our secret fears or fondest hopes. Mine were always the same, placing her at the center of my universe, the object of my dreams. The thought of losing her was my deepest dread. When she told me her dreams, they always made me sad; I got a funny feeling in my throat that wouldn't let me swallow, and I bit my lip to keep from crying. Her dreams never included me.

She insisted that what we did remain an absolute secret. To keep it a secret was something that I regularly and religiously had to swear to. "Say it, Matty," she said.

"No, Leighanne, this is silly, I'm not going to tell anyone."

And she repeated, "Please say it."

"No."

"Matty, you know how sometimes I can make you so excited that when I ask you what your name is you can't remember? If you say it I'll make you forget your name."

"Swear to God. Hope to die, stick a needle in my eye."

I paused momentarily and then continued, "Catch your penis in your fly."

"Don't be obnoxious," she would chide. "Now, you can't ever tell anyone."

She became the most sought-after girl in our district. I'd like to think that if other boys had known she was in love with me, they wouldn't have asked her out, but I'm sure they would have anyway. When anyone else was around, she treated me as if I were a little brother or a best friend, and for her sake, I played my role in the charade. She accepted a date once a week from an older boy, rarely the same one twice. She always insisted on meeting her date in her own car. When they said goodnight, she drove past my house and waited for me, and we would go to the little church and make love with a frenzy.

Sometimes she cried and said that she couldn't understand the way she felt about me or why it was happening to her. She said that to see someone younger than she was unnatural, and probably even against the Lord's will, but that she couldn't seem to stay away from me. I was completely in love with her.

The most eloquent of the nine muses had smiled on me, and I spent hours composing poems to Leighanne. Sometimes I timidly, with red face, offered one for her probable ridicule. When she read it and cried instead of laughing, I knew that, somehow, some way, I would one day make her see that it was me she wanted as the essence and center of her universe.

CHAPTER 9

Christmas

THE HUNTING SEASON WENT BY TOO QUICKLY THAT YEAR. We hunted with people from many walks of life and I liked the work. Each night the night winds whispered things to me that no one else heard. The winds sang Leighanne's song. They caressed the trees with gentle fingers. The sounds roused things hidden deep inside me that reminded me I was unwanted by Leighanne, and not needed by anyone else.

If the hunting guests had never been hunting before, and had never shot a shotgun prior to the time the Colonel invited them to the plantation, Nate would place pen-raised birds in specific locations and throw cracked corn around the spot to keep the birds from roaming until he could return with the hunters. The pen-raised birds that weren't scared to death when the hunters got through shooting could then live a full life in the wild and Nate wouldn't bother them again. One day when I was helping Nate, our guests were two hunters who had never picked up a shotgun before they got here. They worked for General Electric, and the Colonel was trying to get a defense subcontract from their company. Nate got their attention. "Gentlemen, you will observe the tree about two hundred meters away, the one with the white paint on it. I believe that a covey of birds will be found there. Remember the lessons you received at the clay-pigeon range, and don't shoot if in doubt."

The two funny guys with thick glasses sat there. "Gentlemen," Nate said, "please dismount and follow the dogs. I believe they will point at that tree."

When one of them shot the dog box on the back of the wagon, Nate dropped to the ground and crawled under the wagon. I did the same. I looked toward the back of the wagon, and the covey of quail had run under there with us. I didn't blame them, but I lay there praying that the shooters didn't know they were here.

In November after Patty and I got promoted to assistant hunting guides, we were riding with Chief one day. One member of the hunting party named Mr. Bledsoe had recently had some serious heart problems and almost didn't live. After a fairly respectable covey rise kill, Patty and I were gathering the four downed birds. Mr. Bledsoe said to anyone listening, "By gosh, this is exciting. I'm glad I brought my nitroglycerin pills."

"I thought nitroglycerin was used to blow things up," Patty said.

Mr. Bledsoe chuckled and told Patty, "I've taken enough to blow up a small bridge since my heart attack."

Fool Patty then asked Mr. Bledsoe, "What do you think would happen if you killed three birds on a covey rise?"

"I expect it would put a strain on my heart, to say the least."

The fool then tells the man, "If you killed three birds on a covey rise and had an orgasm at the same time, you probably wouldn't live through the experience, would you?" I used to wonder what he thought about, walking home alone all those times.

The next week both of us had to walk home from the far corner of the plantation. Again, we were riding with Chief, and one of the dogs squatted to do its business just exactly as Patty had seen them do one trillion times. He looked up as if he had just discovered the theory of relativity and said loud enough for everybody in the hunting wagon to hear, "Matty, you ever thought why dog crap is tapered at the end? I'll tell you why; it's to keep the dog's asshole from slamming shut." Chief looked at Patty and he got off the wagon, and when I laughed he turned around and looked at me, and I got off and walked home with Patty.

The last time I rode on the wagon that season with Chief was two weeks later when Patty was along. This time one of the Colonel's attorneys and a banker that he did business with were in Chief's hunting party. When Patty found out what their professions were, he told them, "My Uncle Charlie said that a damned lawyer or banker ought not to be allowed to be buried in the same cemetery with decent folk."

We stopped and fought twice that day while we were walking home. From that day forth, if Patty wanted to go, I wouldn't ride because I knew he'd do something or say something and Chief would make us walk home.

When we got home that afternoon Uncle Charlie met us at the door and announced, "You'll be happy to know that your Aunt Mary and her family are coming here for Christmas. I got a letter today, saying that she had a surprise to tell us."

"Does this mean Shithead's coming with them?" asked Patty.

"Don't call your cousin names, Patty. He's my nephew just like you and Matty are. I'm the only one allowed to call him Shithead."

"What did she say the surprise was about?" I asked.

"She wrote that it had something to do with their

hundred-acre farm and Standard Oil Company. My guess is that they struck oil on the place. She ain't going to let me get Laurice in a poker game, that's for sure."

They drove into our yard the next week. A brand new, yellow Fleetwood Cadillac with a six-foot-wide set of longhorn cattle horns affixed to the front of the hood, pulled a shiny new aluminum travel trailer. A big Harley-Davidson motorcycle was strapped to the rear of the Airstream trailer. Sam Houston drove. I suspect that Uncle Laurice had succumbed to pressure a short distance away and had allowed him to show off by driving the remaining distance to our house. When S.H. hit the brakes in front of our house, the big silver Airstream slammed the rear end of the car and Sammie panicked. Alternately hitting the brakes and the accelerator, he made the rig bunnyhop several yards across the loose sand before Uncle Laurice began slapping him behind the head with his open hand.

When the unruly car settled to a stop, the front doors opened and my cousin and uncle got out and adjusted their tremendous white cowboy hats. Patty giggled at the ridiculous sight. My aunt got out of the back seat, cowboy boots first, and put on her big hat. I giggled and Uncle Charlie coughed a lot. Uncle Laurice offered Uncle Charlie a cigar.

That night, after a meal that Aunt Hattie had labored

over for hours that afternoon, Uncle Laurice announced, "Sam Houston, go out to our brand new trailer and bring in our new, eight mila-, mealy-, milamitary projector. I want to show Charlie what we've been doing since I found oil on the ranch."

"How many acres is in the ranch y'all own?" Uncle Charlie asked.

"Charlie, out in Texas we ranch owners don't talk acres. It's how many sections you own. I ain't rode all the way across our ranch in some time and I don't recall exactly how many sections it is."

"How many cattle have you got on that ranch?" asked Uncle Charlie.

"Well now, I haven't counted lately." He looked hard at Sam Houston. "How many do you think we've got, son?"

"We've still got the four that we found last year when the livestock truck turned over down the road from the house."

Uncle Laurice glared at Sam Houston then whispered loudly, "Don't show your ignorance by not being able to count."

We watched almost four hours of home movies that night. The scenes jerked and bobbed, weaving from the unknown filmmaker's latest point of interest to the next. You could tell when Sammie was the camera man. The picture would zoom from the sky to a tree then to a steaming pile of horse manure, then to some other object of interest that drifted into his vacant brain cavity and made an impression. One scene from a new reel was obviously filmed by Uncle Laurice. It was filmed from the stands of a high school football stadium. The weather was obviously very cold. Sam Houston sat on the sidelines far below in a red and white uniform. The crack of his broad butt clearly showed between the too-tight bottom part of the uniform and the too-short top part. Every few seconds he would turn toward the camera and wave.

They left the next day in search of a more adventuresome place to spend the big roll of crisp hundred-dollar bills that my uncle frequently flashed.

I asked Uncle Charlie and Patty the next day how they liked the home movies that we were forced to watch the night before. Uncle Charlie grinned and said, "I liked the football game when Laurice took the camera off Sammie and showed all those pretty girls kicking up their legs down on the field."

"Me too," Patty said. "I never have seen outfits like those in Georgia. Flesh-colored, skintight bodysuits with red cowboy hats and red boots, and red miniskirts and little halter tops, man alive. Those bodysuits looked almost like real skin, didn't they?"

"I reckon if one of them cheerleaders ever got gas in them bodysuits like I've heard you two thunder butts get it would blow their cowboy boots slam off."

"Or their hats off, one or the other," Patty added.

The Colonel came to our house that Christmas morning with gifts. He stayed and had lunch under the condition that Patty and I could spend the afternoon with him and have dinner that night. He had no close family and confided in us that day that he considered us to be as close to family as he would ever have.

The day after Christmas I asked Nate about these things, and he mentioned, as if he thought I knew, that the Colonel was my granddaddy. I voiced my opinion of this notion and called him a lying son of a bitch (out of his earshot), but the thought, the possibility, no matter how ludicrous, disturbed me. I finally decided that the only way to get to the truth was to trick Aunt Hattie. She had been born on the plantation a few years before the Colonel, had never left the place, and she knew everything that had ever happened here and most things that hadn't even happened yet. She had kept Patty and me since birth whenever Uncle Charlie needed help. She had scolded and fussed at him, taught him remedies for measles and colds and warts and whooping cough. She had switched us and hugged us and tucked us into fire-warmed covers when there was ice outside, and she had never lied to us, not once.

I approached her. "Aunt Hattie, I heard tell that the

Colonel is my grandfather, and the person who told me made me promise not to tell who they were, but they told me to come talk to you, that you wouldn't want to tell me, but that you couldn't tell me a lie about it."

She looked at me sideways with her bottom lip stuck out, as if she were getting ready to go get a limb off a peach tree and tear my tail up. Then she turned the other way and wouldn't look at me. I pleaded, "Aunt Hattie, please tell me, they swore you'd tell me about it."

After a long pause, she spoke in a low voice that shook slightly, and sounded far weaker and older than her normal high pitch. "Matty, you put your shoes on before you go outside and catch your death. You act like you ain't got a lick o' sense."

She finally said, "I reckon it's about time you knew." She sighed deeply then continued. "When the Colonel was a young man working for his daddy down here one summer, the overseer's daughter was a pretty, flirty, and sassy girl just the right age to get in trouble. Nature took its course between her and the Colonel and she got bigged up. By the time the girl herself, or anybody else, come to know her condition, the Colonel was back up north in college, not knowin' nothing about it. When the girl's daddy found out she was pregnant, he got in touch with the Colonel's daddy. Mr. O'Hearn came down here and spent most of the day talking with the girl and her daddy. The next time the old man let the Colonel come down here, your daddy was four years old and had been adopted by Mr. MacDonald, the overseer, and his wife. Your daddy's natural mother was a senior in some college in California, with her own apartment and a car. The Colonel never did find out that he was your daddy's father, and if you ever breathe a word of what I just told you, I'll get the biggest peach tree switch I can find, and you'll sleep on your stomach till you're eighteen."

I swore I'd never tell a living soul, but several days later, and, as I recall, about twenty minutes before I exploded, I couldn't take it anymore and told Patty.

"I reckon you and that damn old douche bag have both lost your minds." He said if I seriously believed that story, that his suspicions were being proved true. He said he had always believed that when we were still in our mother's belly and dividing things up, he got a disproportionately large share of the brains. Regardless of what Patty said, the next time the Colonel went back up north, I went to the big house, sneaked in through the kitchen, and searched the walls for portraits. In the long hall that divided the six bedrooms upstairs was an inset whatnot with shelves from the ceiling to the floor. On the third shelf from the floor was a picture of the Colonel when he was younger. He looked an awful lot like a picture of my father.

CHAPTER 10

Loss of Innocence

UNCLE CHARLIE OWNED AN OLD BLACK 1941 LINCOLN Mark I convertible, about the size of a Sherman tank. (It was the same car he had driven from Tennessee to the hospital when we were born.) The week after Sammie and his family came for Christmas he bought a shiny new green Oldsmobile 98 that had every conceivable option and gadget on it that General Motors made. He confided in Patty and me that the Oldsmobile was compliments of a visiting group of rich Yankees who thought they knew how to play seven-card stud.

The first day he got his new car, he drove around the plantation until he found Patty and me. He depressed the electric window button and said in his deepest Tennessee drawl, "You gents wanna go for a fancy ride?" and Patty and I pushed and elbowed our way into the front seat with him in the middle and me on the outside. As we rode, Uncle Charlie was nonstop explaining all the utterly amazing things the car could do. He pushed a button and cold air came out of these vents, and he explained about this thing they called air conditioning and said he had bought the very first air-conditioned car the dealer had ever stocked. Then he pushed another button and the radio antenna miraculously came out of the fender. He showed us the "strongest signal seeking" radio button that, when pushed, prompted the glow-in-the-dark indicator slide to go back and forth across the radio face, stopping on the strongest station. He showed us the first-on-any-car-ever cruise control. To add a little sizzle and to complete his gadget tour, he told us that the car even had autopilot. "All you have to do," he said, "is mash the cruise control and the push-button radio selector at the same time, and the car will automatically drive you to wherever that radio station is located. I'm going to tell you boys something. If you believe that all men are created equal, you just wait till you're driving a brand new car and you pass a man walking. You'll damn sure change your mind."

For the next three weeks Uncle Charlie must have taken everybody he knew in Chickasaw County for a ride in that car, showing the same buttons and telling the same lie about his autopilot. He told it so many times that he started believing the story himself. Three weeks to the day after he got the car, Uncle Charlie and his foxhunting buddies got into one of their not infrequent all-night, whiskey-drinking, poker-playing sessions. In the hospital the next day, barely able to laugh about it, he told us that when he started home at five o'clock that morning he was so drunk and sleepy that he was about halfway home before he remembered his car had autopilot. When he remembered, he mashed the cruise control and the radio button at the same time and lay down in the seat and went to sleep.

He said, "Fellers, y'all ain't gonna believe this, I know, cause it's hard for me to believe, but that damn car went almost a mile and a half before it turned over. Hit a big oak I was told. Knocked me cold as a cucumber while I was asleep. Scared me to death when I woke up and this doctor and a whole mess of nurses was standing over me in those white face masks and hats. I thought they was angels. They told me I opened my eyes and said, 'Oh hell, I'm a-dying, or I'm already dead.' One or two of them nurses looked just like angels. Fact is one of 'em is coming in directly to give me a body rub. You boys check the lock on that door on your way out to make sure it locks from the inside."

I asked Uncle Charlie the next day how his body rub turned out.

"Well, Matty, it's near like that book I read by that fellow Shakespeare about Romeo and Juliet. These two boys
named Tybalt and Mercutio got in a knife fight and
Mercutio got stabbed. When Romeo asked him how bad
he was hurt he said, ''Tis not so deep as a well, nor so wide
as a church door; but 'tis enough, 'twill serve.' Now that
body rub 'tis enough, 'twill serve."

After he got out of the hospital, he resumed driving
his more "reliable" Lincoln. "Only 400 Mark I Cabriolets
were built," he told us time and time again.

■ ■ ■

AFTER A FEW WEEKS OF GOING TO TOWN ON SATURDAYS, PATTY
told me that he had figured out what Uncle Charlie did
after he let us out at the movie. "Uncle Charlie is dropping
us at the picture show and then he goes to the bar in the
basement of that big old hotel down the street and gets
himself a whore."

I answered halfheartedly because I really didn't care
what Uncle Charlie did with his Saturday afternoons, and
all I knew was that I wanted to go to the movie. I said,
"Yeah? What business is it of yours what he does?"

Patty had an annoying habit of overexplaining everything. He told me that once there, Uncle Charlie would
negotiate with the bartender, and if he knew the lady and

approved of her, money would be exchanged for a bottle of whiskey and an upstairs room key. If the woman was new and Uncle Charlie had never seen her, the barkeeper would make a call, and a short while later a woman would walk through the bar. Uncle Charlie would either go upstairs with her or wait for the next femme du jour to come to the bar. Some women were independents who tipped the bartender to let them hang around the bar and negotiate their own dates. With these women, though, in order to keep peace with the hotel, the customer would have to rent his own room.

I asked Patty, "How in hell can you speculate about what Uncle Charlie does with such lucid detail?"

He finally admitted, "Uncle Charlie usually tells Nate, play by play, about the wicked things he does every Saturday, thinking they will shock or embarrass him."

"Nate's got a young 'un in nearly every house between here and Albany. I doubt Uncle Charlie is going to shock him."

As a means of either proving or disproving Nate's story, the next Saturday when Uncle Charlie let us out, we were running behind him as fast as we could. His car was in the hotel parking lot, and we nervously walked into the lobby, trying to look as if we had been born in the upstairs presidential suite. Down the hall from the check-in counter was a red neon sign that read "Casablanca Room" and a flashing neon arrow pointing down at a forty-five-degree angle. On the other side of the check-in counter was the elevator, and on the far side of the elevator was a door that had a glass front with what looked like chicken wire inside the glass. Above the door was a lighted exit sign. Printed on the glass, in three-inch red letters, was "Fire Escape." Behind the door of the fire escape was where we went when we heard Uncle Charlie's loud voice. Through the window of the door, we watched as he went to the front counter, escorting a bleached-blonde lady wearing the brightest red lipstick and the tightest red dress I'd ever seen.

He announced in a voice loud enough for us to hear clearly, "Me and my little wife here need a room with a view of the river, please, Percy."

Uncle Charlie was slightly hard of hearing. He thought he had to talk loud in order to be heard.

The clerk behind the counter was a slight man with a thin nose and thinning black hair, which he combed back. He wore horn-rimmed glasses. His thin face wasn't as wide as the polka dot bow tie around his scrawny neck. A prominant Adam's apple bobbed up and down, hiding itself under the polka dots at its lowest point down before bounding up almost to his chin. Red galluses over a white shirt supported black trousers. He sniffed. "Mr. Anderson, I've been working behind this counter going on nine years, and you've been married to a different woman every Saturday since my first day here. Isn't it against the law in Georgia to have so many wives?"

"I was going to tip you twenty dollars this Christmas, Percy, but you have just curdled the milk of human kindness that flows through my body. Don't look for but two dollars from me in your stocking."

The following week, Patty was abnormally quiet and self-absorbed, and I knew without a doubt what was eating a hole in his gut. He suspected that I had had sex, and he couldn't stand to think that I had beaten him to it. Friday he told me, "Matty, I'm fourteen, almost fifteen, and I've never done it with a woman. So I tell you what I'm going to do. Tomorrow when Uncle Charlie lets us out at the movie, I'm going to run around to that hotel, and when he comes out of that bar with that blonde-headed woman, I'm going to jump out and say, 'Aha, you old bastard, I've caught you! Now, if you don't want everybody who lives on that fucking plantation to know what you do every Saturday, then you better tell that lady to let me have some, too.'"

There wasn't a doubt in my mind that Uncle Charlie was going to kill Patty, but I couldn't let him get killed by himself, so I went too.

We ran to the hotel and waited in the fire escape for almost an hour. When Uncle Charlie didn't come out, we decided he must somehow have gotten past us and had already gone upstairs. Patty was going to have to wait another week to get killed. We wandered around outside, hanging around the car, not knowing what else to do. Unexpectedly Uncle Charlie came out the back door, escorting an old woman so ugly she couldn't have given sex away in the freshman dorm of an all-male college, or on a troop ship crossing the Atlantic. He furtively looked in both directions, glad that he didn't see anyone that he knew. Time wouldn't allow us to do anything better, so we quickly got into the backseat of the car and crouched as low as we could, holding our breath and hoping they wouldn't look back.

Uncle Charlie opened the front door for her, walked around the car and got in his side, and as he was starting the car I could hear him saying, "I ain't never heard of no Shriners' Convention, and why in hell did they pick Albany, Georgia? I never would have thought I'd see the day when they wasn't a single available lady in the whole city of Albany. Now, I'm going to tell you something, ma'am. When that bartender and me started talking back there in that bar and I was telling him what awful shape I was in, me wanting a woman so bad and all, and you overheard us and said you would be glad to suck—uh, you know what. Well, I've heard of fellers like that. Up in

Tennessee, we call 'em quares, but I never have, pardon me, heard of ladies that enjoyed doing that to a man. Like I said, up in Tennessee, we call 'em quares. I don't know what they call 'em in Georgia, but I'll tell you this much. Now, I don't think much of the notion of paying good money for a lady to suck, er, you know what—but I want you to know that Charlie Anderson ain't no quare, but hell, pardon me, I'm in awful condition. I tell you this, it's about dark now and I'm going to drive down by the river, and I'm going to let you 'you know what' but I'll tell you one thing. I'm going to get myself two rocks and if you bite my tallywacker, I'm going to clap you on the ears so hard you'll think the bells in St. Joseph's steeple was inside your head. Now you ain't going to bite my tallywacker, are you?"

"No, sir, I'm not going to bite you and I'd be much obliged if you didn't clap me on the ears with any rocks. Er, can I have the five dollars in advance?"

The night was still and voices carried easily. An almost full moon was breaking the eastern tree line across the river. The chorus of ten thousand frogs could be heard echoing from the bottomland along the river. An occasional car light could be seen crossing the bridge a quarter mile up river. Fifteen minutes passed and we heard Uncle Charlie rasp in a strange voice, "Now, this don't mean I trust you entirely, you being a lady quare and all, but I'm going to put these rocks down, and you damn well better not bite me."

The moon had broken the silvery ties the tree line held on it and had paved a moon-colored thoroughfare across the river directly toward me. We heard the plaintiff voice of old Clark Gable, "Lady, I'm going to grab you by your ears, but if I hurt you one little, bitty bit, you just tell old Uncle Charlie."

I imagined the bright moon grinning when a few minutes after that we heard, "Good God from Glory, I ought to be punished this way more often."

The next week was hell for Patty. Again he was withdrawn and quiet. Uncle Charlie eyed him suspiciously all week, trying to put a mental finger on Patty's behavior without having to weasel the reason for the strange mood out of me. I should have known the little son of a bitch was up to something the next Saturday when he told me I could ride in the front seat and he would ride in the back. He never rode in the back seat. About ten miles from town Patty blurted out, "Uncle Charlie, can I go to the whorehouse with you? I'm old enough, and I ain't never done it before."

Uncle Charlie glared at me for not telling him what to expect, then looked around at Patty and said, "Patty, one of these days I'm going to fall over with a heart attack, hearing some of the stuff that comes out of your vile and blasphemous mouth. It's a thousand wonders the good Lord don't strike you down. Even if what you're alluding to were true, you couldn't go with me. What if somebody found out?"

And in a high-pitched voice Patty squealed, "What if they found out about this? 'Lady, I'm gonna grab you by your ears, but if I hurt you one little, bitty bit, you let Uncle Charlie know!'" My heart quit beating. I sneaked a look at Uncle Charlie. His face was as red as a fox's rear end in pokeberry season. I braced myself to get my brains knocked out.

Then Patty begin to plead, "Uncle Charlie, I don't want to go to no picture show this evening. I want to go with you to the whorehouse and get myself a woman." Nothing happened, and I finally breathed.

When Uncle Charlie stopped in front of the movie he said, "Matthew, you get out here. Seems like your brother's ready to kick the traces off. Patty's going with me this evening." He hesitated. "If either of you ever tell Aunt Hattie about this you'll go back to cleaning the dog pens again."

CHAPTER 11

The Nimrods of Echowah

PATTY STRUTTED AROUND ALL THE NEXT WEEK JUST LIKE General Sumter, the gamecock that had survived for six seasons and was now Uncle Charlie's secret weapon in his quest for the perfect cock. The chicken was named after General Thomas Sumter, who was known as the Fighting Gamecock during the Revolutionary War.

Uncle Charlie stopped asking us to go to town with him after that. We settled into a routine that summer. I waited on Saturdays for Leighanne in case she could meet me, and Patty rode into town with Nate or Chief or he hitchhiked into Albany. Press caught Bunk and two of his buddies skinning a deer on the plantation, and Uncle Charlie took him to town to the sheriff's office to attest to the facts and swore out a warrant for Bunk's arrest. Bunk signed his own bond, which he could do because he was a landowner, and never went to jail. Summer slipped into autumn. The Colonel came down early that year in September, several weeks before our fifteenth birthday. He and several of the plantation owners met with the sheriff and they bought an extra patrol car and paid for an additional deputy whose sole duty was to police the roads around the several tracts of land. It seemed as if each time a defensive play was made the poachers increased their slaughter. The deputy caught two men one night shining for rabbit and they confessed that they and several others were selling the game they killed to people in Albany. They paid a fifty-dollar fine and were released.

The next week Nate picked us up after school. "The Colonel wants you to be in charge of the skeet range. I told him you'd probably get someone killed or kill someone yourself. Why he thinks either of you have enough capable sense to do this is beyond me."

"Why's he taking you off that job, Nate?" I asked him.

"I fought with the Colonel in Africa. I am Senegalese."

"He's promoting you?" Patty asked.

"He wants the slaughter to stop. Why he won't let me kill those people I don't understand. He said we had to debate our differences with these people on a more civilized plane."

Guests of the plantation who weren't proficient in the

use of a shotgun, or those who wanted merely to hone their skills, were invited, nudged, or gently persuaded, according to their individual shooting aptitudes, to enjoy a few hours at the shooting range before a plantation hunting guide turned his back to them on a covey point. Patty and I took the assignment the Colonel had given us as shooting instructors in stride. We made the most of it, adding some creative innovations. Other plantations often rendered unto us the sincerest form of flattery—imitation.

We set up a circular course in the woods behind the skeet range and mowed a meandering path next to the course. Behind clumps of weeds we hid ten mechanical clay pigeon throwers and concealed a string pull. A shooter could walk the course and someone following him could activate the trigger mechanism on the thrower by pulling the string. The clay bird would fly from behind the bushes unexpectedly. This was supposed to emulate a single bird getting up wild. Patty and I walked back toward the hay barn after checking our course out a couple of times. He squatted to examine some imaginary thing in the grass, and looking up from his squatting position, asked me, "Who's the best fucking shot on the plantation?"

"Uncle Charlie or Nate, one or the other. There ain't no question about that."

"I'm the best."

I told him I figured that he was about as full of crap as an overweight elephant that had been eating green clover, and walked on toward the barn. He caught up about the time I reached the sunny side of the building. I slid down the barn wall where I fully intended to sit the rest of the afternoon, savoring the soon-to-be-forgotten late fall sunshine, and daydream about Leighanne.

It was late November, the time of year when the rising sun seemed more reluctant to break the bonds the earth held on it. With each passing day the air was crisper in the mornings and less inclined to deliver the pleasing smells of green grass and flowers. Misty fog, mixed with last evening's leaf-burning smoke, often permeated the cool morning air. I was going to meet Leighanne the following morning while her parents were at church, and I wanted the time alone to mentally pen a poem for her.

"Don't you have something else to do?" I asked him.

"Nope. Everybody on the place except Aunt Hattie is pissed off with me for one thing or another. I guess I could go find her and make her mad but I'd rather stay here and make you mad."

We heard a car door slam in front of the barn, and both of us, with the natural instinct that dated back five generations to the Chickasaw maiden that had married my ancestor, slunk up to the clapboards and looked through a crack in the wall. Patty and I both were rail thin with dark hair and skin. Most people who saw us for the first time often speculated that we must have some Indian blood in our ancestry.

We watched through the crack as Uncle Charlie was hiding a five-gallon jug of moonshine whiskey, with an indeterminate proof, under the hay at the back of one of the stalls. Patty said, "So that's where the old bastard hides his 'shine whiskey." We slid back down the wall, and the last bastions of the Hippolates Puso swarmed about our faces, trying to find a wintering place in our ears or nostrils or eyes. I yawned and as was usual, one of the little gnats decided that this was an opportune time to commit suicide by flying in my mouth.

Uncle Charlie had on numerous occasions rationalized his drinking habit thusly, "Boys, the miasma that creeps out of the swamps and attacks a man's system in the summer, and the bitter cold that chills my bones of winter, constitute a menace to one's health that can only be fought off with inward draughts of an outward but spirituous libation. Hell, boys, I can't quit drinking whiskey, because then I would become a slave to my own will power. Besides that, the Bible said in the Book of Proverbs, to 'Give strong drink and wine unto him that is ready to perish or unto those that be heavy of heart. Let him drink, and forget his poverty, and remember his misery no more.'"

Fifteen minutes passed and Patty elbowed me and said, "Matty, I'll bet you all the money the Colonel gives us for Christmas that I'll hit more clay birds than Nate or Uncle Charlie, after they go ten times around that course me and you just built, as long as I can make whatever side bets with either of them I want to."

I figured the warm sunshine of this late fall afternoon had sapped the boy's reason, so I extracted two or three "Swear to God"s before I took him up on his bet. "You've made one foolish bet," I told him as we shook hands.

Patty lazily got up to go find Uncle Charlie and inform him, "Nate's been bragging to everybody on the place that he could outdrink you. He said you were getting too old to hold your liquor. He said, furthermore, he could shoot a shotgun twice as good as you. He said he could even out-shoot you drunk. You're not really getting too old, like Nate said, are you, Uncle Charlie?"

"I can drink as much as any man in Chickasaw County and still walk a straight line, and I can damned well shoot a shotgun with the best there is. I can't believe Nate would make a statement that profoundly foolish."

"Well, you know how he is. Anytime he gets an audience he says things that he don't mean. What he needs is for somebody to show him his limitations." The next morning Patty found Nate down by the stables. The gypsy farrier, who came through every other month shoeing horses and shearing mules, was shoeing Nate's personal horse and Nate was leaning against the stable wall with his arms crossed, comfortably watching. "Hey, Nate, whatcha doing? Uncle Charlie making you hold up the barn wall or something?"

Nate flinched but otherwise didn't acknowledge Patty's presence.

"You still mad at me for stealing the last watermelon of the year off your porch? Hell and damn, the thing wasn't that good anyway."

Nate turned his back so he wouldn't have to look at Patty. "You know what I heard this morning?"

Nate glared at Patty through narrowed eyelids then turned his head slightly and spit at a spot on the barn wall where two houseflies basked in the warm sun.

"I overheard Uncle Charlie telling some of the field hands that Nate's a pretty fair shot, but that he's never seen any French-speaking foreigner who could shoot as good as he could, or hold his liquor as good either."

By that Friday, Patty had conjured up a bet between himself, Nate, and my Uncle Charlie that made me wish I hadn't already decided what I was going to buy Leighanne for Christmas.

Uncle Charlie and Nate were to walk abreast down the path of the clay pigeon course. Each would have a shotgun with one shell in it. Patty would be the pull man.

My job was to reload the clay bird thrower and cock it, making it ready for the next turn around after Patty had pulled the string, releasing a well-hidden clay pigeon. Whoever shot the bird first got to pour the other one a shotglass full of Uncle Charlie's moonshine whiskey. Whoever had killed the most clay pigeons after ten laps around the course would be declared the winner. The loser would shoot first against Patty for two laps around the course, then the winner would go two laps against Patty.

Uncle Charlie backed away slightly and looked Nate up and down, psyching him out. "Nate, you want to give these boys some toting instructions?"

"What do you mean, Mr. Charlie?"

"Nate, you ever drank any of that hooch that I get from old man Miller? It'll make your brain smoke. All I want to know is where you want these boys to tote you; this place ain't exactly within crawling distance of your house."

"Mr. Charlie, in Senegal, where I was born, we drink a mixture of cattle urine and blood, fermented and carried in a animal's bladder. Do you think that this 'hooch' of yours will upset my constitution?"

Uncle Charlie hit the first two birds and, with much ado and ceremony, poured Nate two shotglasses of the devil's own. Watching Nate's expression closely to judge his reaction to the white whiskey, he commented behind his hand to me and Patty, "One of you might ought to think about where the big wheelbarrow is, looks as if we're going to need it to take Nate home. When I beat this fellow it's going to call for an orgasm."

Nate got the next three clay pigeons in a row and, with the most polite (I assumed) French retort, offered Uncle Charlie the same as received. Then in English, "Mr. Charlie, I would be pleased to get Aunt Hattie to cook for the boys for the next several days while you recuperate if you want."

"Nate, you'd stand a better chance of raising the dead, parting the Red Sea, or pissing over the Pope's head than you would of beating me."

The score was forty-five birds for Uncle Charlie; forty-five birds, Nate. Ten clay birds had been missed and peals of laughter had been replaced with grunts and giggles. The score was tied, so a coin was flipped to see who would shoot against Patty first. Uncle Charlie called heads. When I had to tell him and Nate which side the coin had fallen, I realized that the chances of my winning the bet with Patty were in dire straits. I tried to back out of the bet.

The next two rounds between Patty and the Nimrods of Echowah resulted in considerable physical insult for the flora, instead of for the clay birds that Uncle Charlie and Nate shot. Patty could have beat them if he had had a blindfold on. Twenty fallen branches later, Uncle Charlie and Nate crawled to the barn on all fours. The lead constantly changed and occasionally the one in front would turn, and with a crooked grin tell the lagging shooter to "get a move on, can't you hold your liquor? I can outcrawl you any day of the week."

I found them in the barn the next morning, still asleep and snoring so loud that the little wisps of Bermuda grass hay closest to their mouths fluttered with each exhaled breath. Uncle Charlie's head was cradled in the pit of Nate's shoulder. Nate's leg was draped over Uncle Charlie's legs, and they were holding hands. I had the presence of mind to run the hundred yards to the back door of the main house and get the Polaroid camera from Doris Lee. I figured there might be a chance for me to recoup my losses if I threatened to show the pictures. I knew that Patty would spend every cent that the Colonel gave the two of us on himself. I hoped he choked on whatever he bought for himself that Christmas. Well, got sick anyway.

I should have had the presence of mind not to show the pictures to Patty. All I got out of the deal, after he showed them to everybody on the plantation, was a decision by Uncle Charlie to make me stay home the next three Saturdays while he took Patty to town. Nate told me that if any of his girlfriends heard about the pictures I would be well advised to wear clean underwear so the undertaker wouldn't think that I didn't believe in personal hygiene.

Sometimes I hated the little son of a bitch.

CHAPTER 12

Dog Days

THE MONTHS CREPT. WHEN YOU ARE YOUNG AND WAITING for something—you don't always know what—time creeps. Suddenly spring gently shook our land and woke it from the sleep of winter. Daffodil and silver bell had made the air sweet in February, and the Japanese magnolia made it pink. The wisteria had snowed its violet petals from the sinistrose climbing vines that spiraled up tall barren trees. The lion of March yet slept. The last guests had gone from the plantation, and to those of us who lived here full-time that single event was as welcome as the first bloom of the flowering spring. This year the tension felt because of the problems with the poachers had taken the softness off the season and replaced it with an edge.

I told Leighanne for the thousandth time that I loved her and she told me that I was not who she intended to ever love. "You are not my knight in shining armor, Matty. You don't even know who your grandparents were. You have no grasp of the things that are important to me. I want a man who can trace his lineage to the *Mayflower* if that be possible."

"Why is that so important to you, Leighanne?"

"Matty, you have no index. You don't know your origin."

I wanted to tell her that the Colonel was my grandfather. I didn't. I asked Uncle Charlie if he could tell me about our ancestors. He laughed and said, "The ones who didn't die in prison were either shot or hung. Which one did you want to know about?"

She was a senior this year, her last year in our school. She had a natural gift for academics, plus she studied hard. She applied for and received a full scholarship to the University of Georgia. She was the only person I knew who read the *Wall Street Journal*. When we were together her eyes were always brightest when she talked about going away and never coming back to this spot in the road. My Camelot was in her eyes reduced to nothing more than a place to escape from. I had no illusions that she was not sincere, but I loved her enough to rethink my position and start thinking about the day I would have to leave here too if it meant I could be with her.

The March winds lived up to their reputation and debuted like a lion and slipped away like a lamb. Press had never known on what day he was born, so Patty and I had given him April first as his official birthday when we were small. I had ridden into Albany the last day of March with the Colonel, and he and I had picked out a new black saddle and bridle and a bright red saddle blanket for Press's birthday. The gift would be from me, Patty, and the Colonel even though the Colonel paid for everything. I did pay for a red neckerchief to match the blanket. When the three of us drove to deliver the birthday gifts the next morning, Patty was just as excited as I about seeing Press's reaction.

The house they lived in was typical shotgun style. The roof line was an upside-down vee running the length of the house. A small porch was on the front of the structure, and wooden steps led from the clean-swept yard up to the center of the porch. A single board stretched waist-high from the upright posts on either side of the steps and turned ninety degrees at the corner posts and connected to the house. Aunt Hattie had filled the boards with multi-colored vessels, and each was brimming with healthy and profusely flowering plants, mostly petunias. Two elephant ear plants stood guard on either side of the steps. Press had his black horse tied to one of the posts and was vigorously grooming the winter hair from the horse with a stiff brush when we drove up. When the truck stopped, Press called to the house. "Hattie Bell, you got company." He turned to us and smiled and said, "Morning to you, Colonel. What meanness you two boys up to today?"

"We brought you a birthday present, even though you don't deserve one," Patty told him.

"How old are you this year, Press?" the Colonel asked him.

"I guess I'm about your age, Colonel. When I come here looking for work in 1911, your pappy told me he had a son about my age. Said you had just got out of West Point. I recollect him asking had I ever been in the army, and I told him I rode with the 33rd Black Cavalry out west. I must be seventy, maybe seventy-one."

"Come look at what we got you," I told him. When he looked in the back of the truck a grin spread across his face and stayed there until we left sometime later. He gingerly got the saddle and blanket out as if it were fragile and walked toward his horse.

"Look what we got here, Magic. Look what the Colonel and the boys brung us." He saddled the horse and easily slipped the black bridle into its mouth.

Patty asked, "Can I ride Magic, Press? I won't run him."

"Ain't nobody ever rode this horse but me, Patty. I

don't imagine old Magic lettin' anyone else sit on his back." The horse nuzzled Press as if agreeing.

"Please, Press. I can ride that horse just as good as you can."

Chief had turned Press's garden spot with a turning plow a few days before. The ground was soft and smelled good. Rain had made the ground a little muddy.

"You can try, Patty. Lead the horse out in that soft dirt a ways before you get on, though."

The only thing I heard Patty say was a high-pitched "whoa." Magic remained unridden by anyone but Press, and the Colonel wouldn't let Patty ride in the front seat going home. He didn't want him to get mud on his seat covers. Before we left Press, the Colonel had pulled a large envelope from his coat and handed it to him. Press looked at the contents and asked the Colonel what it meant. "I got the Military Review Board to look into the charges against you in Texas. They found that it was self-defense. Nothing's on your record against you." I saw tears in the old black man's eyes when he grabbed the Colonel's hand and shook it.

That spring when I was fifteen was the spring of my discontent. It was a time of anger, of disappointed expectations, of half-grown-up, half-childlike dreams. It was a time when facial pimples seemed far more important than the Russian leader Khrushchev's latest shoe-pounding threats. I had soared happily through the prior months with Leighanne, much like the cicada that emerges after thirteen years of living underground as a larva, not caring that life as a cicada above ground was limited to a few days, only happy that for the moment it could fly. The inevitability of her leaving weighed heavy. The eager anticipation that she felt made it worse.

The month of May arrived, and I sat in the back of our high school auditorium, fanning with a wooden-handled paper fan donated by the local funeral home. I listened to her tell an audience of well-wishers, parents, and grandparents, "To be the recipient of the highest honor bestowed upon a graduating senior is, indeed, an honor. But this is not the end of my personal learning experience." She told everyone within earshot that she intended to pursue her education at the University of Georgia. She told them of her dreams, her hopes, her plans to become a research scientist. She told them of her aspirations to marry a doctor or a scientist, to feed the world's hungry and heal its sick, to create order where there is chaos.

Nothing she said included me. I wanted to jump up and shout as loud as I could. I wanted her to stop saying those things. I wanted to shout, "You love me, Leighanne! I'm the one who makes you sing; I make you laugh. I'm the one who makes your eyes shine, the one who makes you dance barefoot in the meadow! I'm the one who makes you cry because you love me!" I sat there instead, saying nothing, feeling lower than whale shit, and wanting to cry.

The summer was long, hot, and seemed to drag on eternally. She tried harder and harder to stay away, but she always came back. We laughed and made love, and giggled and touched and made love, and she said that she was leaving and not coming back, and on those days I wished that the fast-growing kudzu vines would creep through the cracks in the old house and strangle me while I slept. I lived on a thin red line between ecstasy and agony. The entire summer my moods ebbed and flowed according to her latest whim or her latest declaration of her intentions never to see me again.

That summer, I was either sulking and quiet or moody and brooding. On more than one occasion, I overheard conversations of people on the plantation, explaining my moods and probable reasons for my acting so strange. The analysis invariably concluded that my age was the primary reason for sulking, that all fifteen-year-old post-puberty boys were moody. And just as invariably was the standard rejoinder, "That aggravating little Nazi bastard Patty is fifteen, too, unless he's a midget Auschwitz war criminal in disguise. Why in the hell doesn't he just sulk and brood?"

September came. Dog Days in the South. The first

seven days, according to the old people, always set the climate and rainfall for the ensuing thirty-three days of Dog Days. This was a time when ringworm readily infected the feet of small barefoot children wading in mud puddles left by sudden downpours of late summer. Dog Days were the bad that preceded the good of Indian Summer. Dog Days were when the sassafras, the staghorn sumac, and tupelo raced to see which one would be first to silently announce with brilliant crimson foliage, "Get ready, autumn is coming!" Dog Days were when she left.

She met me in the meadow, small and beautiful and wise, blue eyes misted with tears. She told me, "Don't you see, Matty, it really is for the best. I need to get on with my life, and you need to find someone else and get on with yours."

She told me she would never forget about me, but that she was leaving for school in a few days and would eventually find the man she had dreamed and planned about all her life. She would find one who was brilliant, a scholar, rich and handsome, one from a socially prominent family. A man who owned a tuxedo and knew how to cha-cha and rumba, a man who could order from a French menu with ease, who knew congressmen and called them by their first names.

I spent the next few days lying on my back in my old favorite spot, studying the migrating habits of the orange and black monarch butterfly on its way from a summer in Canada to a winter in Mexico. I spent hours planning how I would murder in cold blood the son of a bitch, whoever he was, that put a hand on Leighanne. For days I walked the woods where she and I had walked. Nights, I sat in the meadow next to the lake and waited for the night to begin its symphony, its night song. The whippoorwill was the maestro. Its haunting call when the sky was red was the baton that signaled to the forest orchestra that the song should begin. The bass of the frogs would then provide the beginning background drum rhythm for the crescendo of thousands of reeds and strings and horns to follow.

Some nights when the air was crisp, I watched a small flock of whooping cranes at the lake. It was not known to me then that the birds lived on the cusp between survival and extinction. On the moon-colored lake, these white cranes flexed their snowy white wings and stabbed the fall air with long dagger beaks. All of these things only embellished my sadness. I imagined myself to be as one with the great geese that flew the flyways over the South in the autumn. When one in the flight had lost its mate for life to a hunter's shot, and the survivor would circle and call, the call of the surviving goose was the saddest sound that I ever heard.

I knew that the Colonel's grandfather was half Indian,

and since the Colonel was my grandfather, this meant that I was part Indian. I felt my spirit as one akin to the elusive red wolf that hunted by night, the red ghost it was called by the old-timers, but when I howled my mating call to the moon-filled night, all that answered was the distant baying of an overimaginative bird dog.

CHAPTER 13

October's Blood

OCTOBER CAME, THE MONTH OF THE HARVEST, THE MONTH when Columbus first sighted America, the month when General Robert E. Lee, on his deathbed in postwar delirium, said his last words, "The battle is over. Let us now strike our tents and go home." This was the month Patty and I would be sixteen. This was normally the month of the first killing frost, the time when the crimson oak would justify its flamboyant name, the season when the shagbark hickory, dressed in the brightest of yellows, would shiver and the gray fox squirrels would hide the nuts that abandoned the sighing tree until a winter's day when food was sparse. It was the time when the little sassafras could claim bragging rights as the most beautiful tree in the forest. The trees bled October's blood.

I saw the old wolf that was my reincarnated spirit self late one afternoon that October. I sat on a log by the lake and he came from behind the dam. His thick fur, already pelted for winter, had the faintest of red hues. He stared at me from his vantage point on the dam. I lifted my hand to let him know that I knew him. That night I heard him call from a far distance and I called back. He answered.

Patty was as frantic as a hungry puppy looking for its momma's lunch basket. All he could talk about or think about was getting his driver's license, which, according to him, meant going to town by himself and picking up women and screwing every night of the week.

Patty's new goal in life was to surpass all documented records of the number of sexual conquests ever had by any man. "Matty, I read that Casanova did it with over eleven hundred women and Don Juan with over a thousand. Did you know that the Baseball Hall of Fame was originally suggested by the first-ever commissioner of baseball, a man by the name of Judge Kenesaw Mountain Landis? And he wanted to reserve a place in history for those exceptional greats of baseball. Now, what I want you to do is to start a Fornicators' Hall of Fame, and there I'll be right beside all the rest of the world's super studs. Matty, can you imagine the mentality of someone who would name their kid Kenesaw Mountain? Hell, I think I'll name my first kid Chattahoochee River MacDonald."

Boy, was he ever wound up tight. I finally got tired of hearing about his intentions and told him, "To my knowledge those damned mules we drive that pull the hunting wagons have never before asked to see any driver's license, and what the hell else do you think you will be driving? I, for one, fail to see any cars parked around our house, except for Uncle Charlie's Lincoln, and my guess is that you can forget about driving that."

He laughed his customary wicked laugh and said, "O, ye of little fucking faith: Mark 8:26."

I asked him what he meant by that, but to tell me in a hurry because God was probably getting ready to put his lights out, and I didn't want to get caught standing next to him.

He explained, "Well, just figure on it. Why else would Nate be talking about cars for the last two weeks? Ever since the Colonel got down here, Nate's been asking me what kind we liked and what color we liked, and two hundred other questions about cars, and you know yourself, Nate ain't never talked about anything but himself, the Colonel, bird dogs, and women."

I said, "Patty, you dumb son of a bitch, you've fallen for the oldest trick ever played on people with birthdays coming up. Do you remember this same time last year? Nate told you he and the Colonel had gone to Albany and that the Colonel had bought us a brand new 1959

Chevrolet convertible for our fifteenth birthday, and you fell like a brick for that lie."

He replied, "Yeah, I remember. I also remember when we didn't get the car Nate said that the Colonel changed his mind because we put those two polecats under the main house and provoked them into spraying. Hell and damn, the smell wasn't that bad." I said that the smell was bad, too, and that for the life of me I couldn't remember being with him when he put those polecats under the main house. "You even believed Nate when he told you that the Colonel went back and told the dealer he wanted the car stored until we got sixteen. Now you've fallen for Nate's crap again." Patty got livid, thinking about the possibility of its being true, and stalked off. I was convinced to go look for Nate.

Monday, October 17, 1960, dawned. Helios emerged from the eastern horizon, driving his chariot through reds as bright as the fires of hell. The God of the Sun reluctantly rose, replacing the anger of reds that first showed on the horizon with softer pinks and yellows. With each successive leap toward heaven he molted the sky from indigo, to purple, to perfect blue.

As Uncle Charlie would say, "This is a bluebird morning, boys, a bluebird morning."

For me, the day was only another opportunity to grieve and mope because Leighanne was gone. For Patty, it was a day to run hot and cold all over. Would we get a car or not get a car? We walked to the crossroads to wait for Mr. Calhoun to get there with the school bus so we could tell him some lie about having to stay home that day. By the time he closed the doors and drove away, exposing the spot where we had been standing, we were in the woods and out of Uncle Charlie's suspicious line of sight. For a quarter of a mile through the woods, then out onto the main road toward the plantation's main house, neither of us spoke. You could tell Patty was excited. He was in too much of a hurry to walk, but didn't want to run. Every so often he would skip for a few steps then back step until I caught up.

At one point, halfway to the main house, he stopped and looked up at the sky and the trees as if seeing them for the first time in his life and said, "Boy, Matty, did you ever see a prettier day? I'll tell you what, if I owed somebody a pretty day, and they wouldn't accept today as payment, the son of a bitch wouldn't ever get paid. A day like today almost makes your dick hard, don't it, Matty? Man, look at those red trees. Looks just like the trees are bleeding." So far as I can remember, that's about as close as Patty ever came to complimenting anything.

We hung around the main house and kitchen until Doris Lee suggested that she might need some help, then we hung around the stables. Then we found Nate and

Chief, and we hung around some more. Nobody said anything at all about our birthday, and Patty was becoming more and more agitated and frustrated with each passing hour. I personally didn't care. I was still working on a plan to kill the man (without having to serve hard time in the state penitentiary) who was lucky enough to touch Leighanne. She would naturally suspect me, so this was really going to take some planning. I wished I could ask Patty's advice. He probably already had the perfect murder down pat. The day had remained a perfect fall day and the sun was red and almost down when we finally walked back toward our house. To me, the finale was fully as spectacular as the beginning, but to Patty the day wasn't nearly as pretty as it had been that morning.

We were almost home when the Colonel drove up beside us and asked if we'd like a ride home. On the way he reached into his pocket and gave each of us a fifty-dollar bill, murmuring an apology for not buying us a more personal present. We thanked him, and as we were exiting the truck, he invited us to go to Albany on Saturday with him and Nate. He said he would drop us off at the state patrol station for our license exams while he took Nate to get a truck he had bought for the farm.

That night I lay in my bed planning the murder of Leighanne's future boyfriend, and Patty lay in his planning Nate's murder for lying to him about us getting a car.

Around midnight I rolled on my side and propped my head on one elbow. I knew he was awake. "Patty, if you wanted to kill someone and nobody know it was you, how would you do it?"

"Why would you want to kill someone and nobody know it was you? What you want is for everybody to know it was you, but not be able to prove it. The way I'm going to kill Nate is to tell him that Chief's wife has the hots for him, then when that horny son of a bitch makes a pass at her Chief's going to kill him for me." He paused for a moment then continued, "Mail him a rattlesnake, the postage to Athens can't be that much. Be sure to punch some holes in the box though; the last one I mailed to Nate suffocated."

On Saturday, a little before noon, we walked up to the main house and our designated appointment. We got there early so we could eat in the kitchen. When I knocked on the back screen door, Doris Lee (the best cook in the universe) answered the knock, smiled at me, frowned at Patty, and said, "The Colonel told me you boys might drop by for lunch. He said to tell you he would be a few minutes late. He's having lunch with Mr. Bickerstaff. Now, Matty, you come on in and tell your brother he can come in, too, but if he gooses me one more time, I'm going to slap him in the mouth with a frying pan."

Mr. Bickerstaff owned the neighboring plantation

and was about the same age as the Colonel. He had been a practicing attorney at an earlier time in his life. He told the Colonel that he quit the profession when it became obvious that all honor had fled the field of law. He said, "John Mortimer, a Scottish barrister, called practicing law 'a crude and brutal business.' When it also became a dishonest livelihood, I decided to pursue my avocation. I decided that cattle would make better company than that of my colleagues."

He and the Colonel had been friends since they were young men, and they visited each other now at least once a week when the Colonel was down south. How they sat for hours across a chessboard from each other was beyond me. Mr. Bickerstaff's place was about half the size of our plantation, and the major portion of that was devoted to pasture or grazing land. Mr. Bickerstaff lived and breathed cattle, and his obsession in life was to develop the perfect crossbreed, able to tolerate the heat and humidity of the Deep South and to obtain the optimum feed-to-weight-gain ratio, on diets ranging from scientifically formulated food rations to blackjack oak and bramblebush. The first-generation calves in his breeding program were always one-half Brahma—the Brahma being the sire of the offspring, and the dam being every other species of the bovid family known to man. The reasoning behind this was that the Brahma had sweat glands, a physical characteristic unique to its kind. Hopefully this genetic trait would be passed on to the offspring and make them more tolerant of the climate. His bull pasture was a menagerie of everything from African water buffalo to American bison from Montana. Rare was the time when one rode by and didn't see bulls fighting.

When Mr. Bickerstaff left, with an invitation extended by the Colonel for a return dinner and chess engagement that evening, the Colonel sent for Nate. Nate drove, and the Colonel sat in the front passenger side. Patty stared sullenly out the window still contemplating Nate's demise, while I daydreamed about Leighanne's naked body.

We took the written part of the driver's license test, barely passing. Nate and the Colonel waited outside, having had to change their plans, because we needed the car for the driving portion of the test, which we also barely passed. We then drove downtown to the Chevrolet-Oldsmobile dealership to get the farm truck. Out in front of the dealership was the shiniest, prettiest, goddam reddest 1959 Chevrolet convertible that I had ever seen, and the top was already down. He turned toward us with an ever-so-slight smile, then handed each of us a set of keys and said, "These keys fit the car that I figured both you boys would want. Now, if I ever hear that either of you acted the fool, or risked your own lives, or endangered anyone else's, you will be expected to park that car until you regain the good sense that I suspect is in your genes somewhere. Now, Nate, I'm going to ride back to the plantation with these gentlemen if they will allow me, so you take your time getting home, and thank you for driving us."

Patty jumped out of the back seat, snatched open the front door, hugged Nate, and yelled back over his shoulder on a beeline to the convertible, "I wasn't really going to kill you!" Nate just shook his head in wonder as Patty came as close as he ever has to praying, his prayer being that the key would fit that convertible. That afternoon, with the top down, the Colonel in the back seat, me driving and Patty wanting to, the three of us came awfully close to admitting that we loved each other. I came very close to blurting to the Colonel that he was my father's real daddy. I knew that Patty would kill me though.

About halfway between Albany and the plantation was the Plantation Sportsman's Club, a beer joint located at the end of a wedge-shaped spit of land that was a part of the county that lay between our county and Dougherty County, of which Albany is a part. Only about three hundred yards of the main highway passed through the middle county, where the joint was located. This left it out of the jurisdiction of the sheriff's department of either of the adjoining counties and inaccessible to the home sheriff unless he went through the neighboring counties first.

The Colonel had once said, "Whenever authority is absent, lawlessness prevails."

The patrons of this particular beer joint didn't dispute that particular axiom one bit. Bunk Bartlet and every other man that we suspected of poaching at the plantation used this joint as a hangout.

About a mile away from the Plantation Sportsman's Club, the Colonel shouted above the radio and wind noise, "Matty, when you reach that establishment that sells beer, pull aside. I'm out of beer, and Bickerstaff is dropping by tonight." The Sportsman's Club was the roughest, meanest place in the universe as far as I was concerned, and the only way it ever survived the wrath of the local landowners was through the Colonel's repeated refusals to join the opposition and his voiced opinion against interference with free enterprise each time the subject of closing the place was broached.

I felt really sick watching the Colonel walk through those doors, where animosity against the wealthy landowners was at almost fever pitch, and where on late Saturday afternoons tattoos and motorcycles were the norm, not the exception. This was where picking noses and scratching crotches were accepted etiquette, and where I wouldn't have gone even if Nathan Bedford Forrest and his Tennessee Volunteers had been with me. When he got out of the car, I pleaded with him not to go in there. "Colonel, Patty said that he and Nate just drive to the back door and blow the horn and the owner brings them what they want. Let's please do that."

"Is that a fact? Well, I think I'll speak to the proprietor and see what we can do to curtail your brother's and Nate's equivocation," the Colonel answered, as he walked toward the front door.

Through clenched teeth Patty seethed, "The normal, average, head-out-of-the-ass person thinks three times faster than he talks. Damned if you don't talk three times faster than you think."

The Colonel came out with his bag and got into the car. "Do you men recognize any of the patrons? Is this the place Bunk Bartlet and his friends patronize?"

"Yes sir."

We drove quietly back to the plantation, each of us with his own private thoughts.

CHAPTER 14

The Tamer of the Beast

LEIGHANNE CAME HOME ALMOST EVERY WEEKEND AND told me the same things again about her hopes and aspirations, and we made love. I wrote little messages with my finger on her bare skin, and she laughed with glee when she guessed them, and on Sundays she cried and said she couldn't understand why this was happening to her, and why on earth I didn't just leave her alone, so she could get on with her life.

Days turned into weeks, and these into months. The seasons changed, as did Leighanne and I. In many ways we were as alike as two raindrops that fell from the sky. We were different in that I fell to earth and she fell into a stream that fed a river that made its way to the sea. She was part of a vastness now that I wasn't privy to. I read everything I could to make myself more a part of her world, but it was like trying to learn ballet from an instruction book. I even read a book on etiquette, but Uncle Charlie didn't have the service required to practice where your wineglass and butter knife went in a place setting.

Spring came and went, then came again, and the tiny grosbeaks came once more to south Georgia to mate. The males flashed their brilliant red neckerchiefs in courtship, flirting until some female without the colorful ascot responded. Then they flitted in the brush until a marriage was consummated. When the baby finches learned to fly and the heat became intolerable, they would disappear again for the year.

Leighanne worked and went to summer school sessions, and my body would ache for her when she skipped a weekend and didn't come home. I worked hard on the plantation so that my tiredness would help me sleep at night. Patty did only what he absolutely had to do.

I told Uncle Charlie that I didn't think it was fair for us to get paid the same amount of money when I did the most work.

He said, "Fair? There ain't no such thing as fair. If there was, somebody would erect some big statues of pigeons in the parks so that all the dead Civil War generals and war heroes could come shit on them."

Our eighteenth birthday came with little notice. I got a card from Leighanne with a tiny wildflower pressed between the pages, and I waited that Saturday by the lake to unwrap the package she said would be in red, which she was. She told me she was almost ready to end this relationship because it was not good for either of us.

The first killing frost came that week, and the blackbirds came in noisy hoards and ate what the harvesters had missed. I imagined these gross, noisy birds as not being unlike the Huns with Attila at their head—noisy and destructive. The little killdeer also came from out of nowhere with the frost. They scurried away from the Huns on long skinny legs and protested with their high, shrill voices.

I often heard Uncle Charlie speculate as to how many species had been driven to extinction by the greed of the blackbirds.

The Colonel came for the hunting season and stopped at our house to wish us a belated happy birthday. He hesitated when he started to leave, and I could see that something weighed heavy on his mind. He asked if we could ride with him for a while. He needed to say some things.

"You're eighteen now and I'm afraid you may be called on to do what men have done since recorded history, and I'm being selfish because I want you to stay little boys. There's an ideological conflict over in Southeast Asia that's going to escalate into a full-fledged war for our country, and I don't want you men to get any misguided ideas that there's honor and valor in war. War is cruel and dirty. When the time comes, I don't want you to go."

Patty chimed in, "Nate seemed to enjoy it. He told me and Matty that General Patton promised to piss in the Rhine before the Russians did. He said that if those men in charge had let you and him take over that you wouldn't have even slowed down at the Rhine. He said y'all would have pissed on the Kremlin steps."

"That may be true, Patty, but most men, including myself, came home with an overwhelming hatred for war. They joined the VFW and drank beer with their buddies and talked about Argonne and the Bulge and Inowetok. Some of them still take out their mothball-smelling uniforms each year and march in Memorial Day parades. Some of them still cry and have nightmares at night, and some of them still reach for missing limbs. Believe me, they hate war."

The week of Thanksgiving she came home, and I saw her ride by our house several times, always looking straight ahead as if she didn't know I existed. I walked to the lake each day and called her name. The black gum trees on the far shore, with their midnight purple leaves, shook their boughs in the fall air almost in defiance of the season. They fought to hold on to their foliage long after their less resolute neighbors succumbed to the harsh demands of the autumn winds. The songbirds that normally woke the mornings were songless now. I knew that they missed her too.

On Saturday, the day before she was to return to school, she was waiting for me when I came to the lake. We walked wordlessly across the dam and into a sparse stand of trees. I sat on a fallen pine that had been struck by lightning several years before. The round holes attested that its massive trunk had provided a nesting place for several generations of red-cockaded woodpeckers while it rotted in place, then when it finally gave up and could stand no longer, it fell to the forest floor and the denizens of the understory moved in to render it back to the land from whence it came. She lay on her back in the thick brown grass. Soft hair, the color of summer wheat, framed her pretty face.

"Matthew, you need to get on with your life. You need to forget about me and find someone else."

"Leighanne, you are my life. You're the breath I breathe."

Almost angrily she said, "No, I'm not! Matty, you're not what I'm going to spend the rest of my life doing. I don't want to live down here. I am not going to be a farmer's damned baby factory. I don't even want to come back here for the weekends. Please tell me that you don't want me to come home any more."

"If you'll wait for me, I'll ask the Colonel to lend me the money so that I can go to medical school. I'll be a doctor. I'll be the best damned doctor on the face of the earth. I'll give you the things you want. I'll learn to dance and order from a French menu. I'll move to Atlanta and get to know the governor. I'll even *be* the governor one day."

"Will you please shut up and make love to me, Matthew?"

A single crow sat in the high bare limbs of a tree nearby and voiced his objections to what we were doing. In the distance I heard the red wolf calling his mate.

Uncle Charlie and his foxhunting friend Lem disappeared the next week. Lem wore many hats; one of them was driving the hearse for the funeral home in Spytown, about ten miles away, whenever there was a funeral or when a body needed to be picked up from out of town. He came by our house the Monday after Thanksgiving. "Charlie, you want to ride down to Tampa with me to pick up this old lady. I'll either buy the whiskey and the meals, or I'll split what I'm getting and we'll half the accessories."

"It's according to whether you're going to budget the accessories or not."

"You pick the whiskey and the places we eat."

"That'll serve."

When they didn't get back on Wednesday with the body, the funeral home owner panicked. He couldn't find them or his hearse and he had a funeral to perform. The family had assembled and were expecting a nice but inexpensive ceremony the next day. Seems as if she had saved her money fastidiously, and the relatives wanted to get to the reading of the will as quickly as possible.

The funeral director took a chance and assumed that no one would want to view the remains. He put cement blocks in an empty casket, borrowed a hearse, and charged the family eighteen hundred dollars for the funeral.

The two fox hunters drove into Spytown the next day with the body, and late that night a private ceremony was held and cement blocks were exchanged for the real thing.

I asked Uncle Charlie what happened. "Well, Matty, old Lem was drunk by the time we got to Live Oak. I was forced to drink the balance of the liquor, strictly in order to keep him from getting drunker. We sold the hearse in Chiefland and took a taxi to Tampa. When the folks down there wouldn't release the body to us, I don't mind telling you I was plum ashamed of myself. I sobered up, and with the last ten dollars we had, I bought myself a cigar, a newspaper, and I went to the horse tracks and won enough money to buy the hearse back. I drove back, 'cause Lem's still drunk."

He waited for me to take up for him, and when I didn't, he defended himself, "It ain't altogether my fault that I succumb to spirituous drink without putting up a fight. We transplanted Scotsmen get a taste for the strong drink through our mother's milk and never do learn to master it."

It was a few days before Christmas and Leighanne was home for the holidays. She found me at the kennels and told me that her parents were leaving the day after Christmas to visit relatives in Kentucky, and like a blushing bride not able to look her lover in the face, she asked, "Matty, will you stay with me at my house until I go back to school on the second of January? Mom and Dad are going away and I told them I would get Cindy to stay with me. If you can stay with me, I'll tell them a lie."

"If I have to feed Patty and Uncle Charlie to the piranha I'll stay."

"Why would you do that?"

"When I was younger I would daydream about being the dictator of South America and you being my love slave. I always assumed I'd feed Uncle Charlie and Patty to the fish in the Amazon River."

"Just feed Patty to the fish. I like your Uncle. All the girls think he's sexy."

I needed some help, but I couldn't break my promise to Leighanne not to tell anyone about us. I told Patty I had met a girl and needed to be gone seven days and nights. I asked him if he could think of a plausible excuse for my being gone. He didn't say anything, so I figured the answer was no. The next day, the Sunday before Christmas, Uncle Charlie and I were sitting down to eat. Patty was characteristically late. Perfectly timed, at precisely the moment we finished passing each dish around for a serving, Patty walked in and said, "Matty, I just ran into the Colonel. He's going up north tomorrow for the holidays, and he's scared somebody might break into the big house while he's gone. He said if I'd stay there night and day from the twenty-sixth until the second of January, he'd give me one hundred dollars. I'll let you do it if you want to, if I get to use the car by myself for a month. Dinner looks good, Uncle Charlie. Give the dog mine; I ate with Aunt Hattie."

I should have known Patty wouldn't do anything for anybody if there weren't something in it for him. I was just glad he didn't know how many months he could have gotten. I had saved my money for years, carefully guarding my hiding place from Patty, whose viewpoint on money was, "It's nothing more than a means of exchange, no more, no less. Now, if you don't exchange it, what damn good does it do anybody?" On the twenty-sixth I took five hundred dollars, which was almost all I had, and a small suitcase, and Patty left me on the steps of the locked and vacant big house.

I walked up the entrance road from the house to the main road, and she was waiting.

"Well, what do you want to do first?" I asked, grinning from ear to ear.

"I think it's illegal to do what I want to do in a public highway."

"Where can we go?"

"We can go to my house, silly. I'll race you getting naked."

I won.

The next seven days were utterly incredible. We bathed together; we cooked together; we fed each other. I wrote poems for her. She laughed at the silly ones and cried when she read the ones that described how I felt for her. We sneaked into Albany, she with heavy makeup, I with her father's narrow-brimmed hat. We showed fake IDs and drank beer with whores and old men looking for whores. We hid in a dimly lit corner of the Casa Blanca Room one night and watched the Clark Gable of Echowah Plantation work his magic on a lonely married woman visiting relatives. She stopped the car one night at an auto repair shop closed for the night and we searched the ground for old spark plugs. I took the copper rings off the spark plugs and we put them on our left ring fingers and checked into the big hotel. The desk clerk was the same man on duty when Patty and I had hidden in the fire escape and Uncle Charlie had rented a room. He waited until I had paid the eight dollars for the room then nodded toward Leighanne's hand. "Is that an eighteen-carat Delco, or AC?" I understood why Uncle Charlie had given him only two dollars that Christmas.

One moon-filled midnight, our fifth night together, Leighanne asked, "Matty, have you ever seen the ocean?"

"No."

"Will you write a poem for me about the ocean?"

"Yes."

"Will you drive me to the ocean, and when the sun comes up will you read the poem to me?"

"No, Leighanne, we've been drinking and it's too far. Why don't we just go home?"

"If you'll take me I'll make your eyes cross and make you forget your name."

Four hours later we were climbing the barrier dunes, the sands that daily fought a totally defensive battle against the Atlantic Ocean, a cruel and formidable foe. At night the dunes' enemy is completely a paradox, a marriage of opposites. A vastness of black, building and swelling, preparing for the battle, this monstrous blackness remains its ominous doomsday color until it gets within striking distance of the fragile dunes. At the last possible moment, it seems, the blackness crests and transforms itself into a lacy delicate whiteness, beautiful but deadly. On a seemingly deserted Jekyll Island, I must have looked pretty silly seeing the ocean for the first time. Nothing can prepare a person for their first sight of the ocean. When you were born a long distance from the ocean, and this strange fulfillment that some distant genetic pattern shouts for you to return to manifests itself, the experience is so moving that you almost feel afraid. This ocean and this moment were indelibly printed in my brain. I thought that my dying mental image would be the full moon highlighting her blond hair and the ocean behind her. She laughed, like the tinkling of a music box, as she watched my expressions. We wrapped up in blankets and held each other close, and when the sky turned red, I got up, and with a blanket around me, as if I were the Knight Tristan, I said to her:

> You're my rivers, streams, my oceans,
> My mountains, fields, my plains.
> You stay while others flee my screams;
> You're the saneness that remains.
> You are my time, my distance,

My beginning, my now, my end.
You strum my heart, my mind, my soul;
You're my lover; you're my best friend.
With smiles you turn my tears to poems,
You make my soul burn bright.
You're the keeper of my lighthouse
You guide me through dark night.
You're the reason I've chosen for living,
The alpha and omega of my life,
And if we never speak the vows,
Always, you'll be my wife.
As sure as God's loins spawned the sun
That's breaking in the east,
You calm my seas; you quiet my storm;
You're the tamer of my beast.

When I bowed, she was crying. We wrapped up very carefully and held each other tightly until the sky was blue and the sun was a long way from the horizon. The tiny sandpipers were double-timing, then marking time before plunging their long beaks into the wet sand, always coming out with a tiny crustacean before repeating the process. The gregarious gulls were loudly protesting our presence. The Atlantic Ocean was incessantly pounding its powerful fists against the sands of the barrier island. It reminded me of a news serial I had seen one Saturday, when a tired and obviously beaten heavyweight challenger could only hold his arms in front of his face and wait for the punch he knew was coming.

We drove home in silence. She seemed angry with me and with herself, so I said nothing. This was December 31, 1962, and this day and this night would be our last together for a long, long time. She got drunk that night on champagne, and when Lawrence Welk and his orchestra began to play Auld Lang Syne, she kissed me, and for the first time since I had known her, she shyly and sadly said, "Matty, I love you very much," and we made love for a long time that night, then slept much of the morning.

When we awoke, she was resolute and far more firm than she had ever been. I thought that at midnight last night I must have been the focus of her silent resolutions, and I knew the stars were about to fall from my heaven. She said that I must leave. She told me that she did not want to be in love with me. She told me that she did not want me to love her.

CHAPTER 15

The Weight of the Earth

IN 1567, DON QUIXOTE, BY WAY OF CERVANTES' QUILL PEN, said, "As a grandmother of mine used to say, 'There are only two families in the world, the haves and the have nots.'" I didn't fight windmills as did Don Quixote, but I certainly knew which family I belonged to. I knew every niche in Leighanne's mind and body, and I knew that she had made up her mind. I knew that my idea of hell was about to manifest itself.

I felt as if I were Icarus. With wax and feather wings, fleeing from King Minos's island of Crete, I had gotten too cocky and sure of myself and had flown too close to the sun and my wings had melted. There were amazing similarities between Greek legend and south Georgia reality. With a terrible abruptness I came down to earth.

The weight of the earth was calculated by an English scientist named Henry Cavendish in 1798. His calculations were amazingly accurate, and I felt as if all 6,595 million million million tons were weighing me down as I walked the back roads that would take me past the quarters and on to the main house. She saw me coming from her kitchen window and ran the distance to meet me, "Lord, child, tell your Aunt Hattie who's done this to you, and I'll make them rue the day they was born." I stayed and ate with her and her husband: the New Year's Day traditional fare of black-eyed peas, hog jowl, and collard greens. Then the chemical that numbs your brain when pain is overwhelming took over, and as she had done so many times in my life, Aunt Hattie tucked me into sweet-smelling sheets that had been hung on a line and dried by the sun. I slept the sleep of the dead, until the smell of bacon and eggs shook me awake the next morning.

"Aunt Hattie, I know you believe in hexes and spells and secret potions. Could you teach me how to cast a spell on someone?" I asked as I was leaving her house.

"Matty, the spells and hexes the black folks use are meant to cause harm and misery. I've raised you and I know there's not a bone in your body that wants to harm another being, so you must be talking about some sort of love potion. Son, there ain't one. If the girl has got any sense a'tall she'll come back."

Walking home, I remembered a line from a poem Leighanne had read to me in the meadow, by John Greenleaf Whittier. "Of all sad words of tongue or pen, the saddest are these: It might have been."

The old women around the plantation whispered, "It's just his age," and someone else would whisper, "His bastard brother is the same age."

If time is the great healer for pains of the heart, January, February, and March of 1963 indicated that my convalescence would be long and painful.

That spring, the days seemed less reluctant each morning to break the bonds the night held on them. The comfort of darkness was what I sought, and the willingness of the sun to light the earth was a thing that angered me to no end. The spring should postpone itself until she came back to me. No one should be alone in the spring. The narcissus and daffodil had made their showy appearance in mid-January, filling the air with the sweet smell of the earth coming to life anew. The risk takers, the silly plum bushes and peach trees, had burst forth in bloom, daring the last footprints of winter to prune them as it usually did. The wise old white oak sat barren and waiting, with its fruit held in stay, for the final sign of winter, the cold spell the old-timers called blackberry winter. Forget-me-nots bloomed on the side of the hill. The legend behind that name dated to medieval times when a suitor leaned too far over a cliff to pick the blue flower for his lover, and as he fell to his death he beseeched her, "Forget me not."

Uncle Charlie contended that trees need the harsh and powerful March winds to flex and stretch their trunks and branches so that sap could more readily draw up to nourish the tender budding leaves. He said that people were similar; that adversity strengthened the soul. I was probably going to be a Tibetan monk.

I soliloquized Notchawahatchee Creek as "The Styx." Hell continued unabated, and with a vengeance. When I was a child I asked Uncle Charlie what the Indian word "Notchawahatchee" meant. He said that he wasn't positive, but he thought it meant "Enter this swamp and you can kiss your white ass goodbye."

April 1 arrived, and I walked to Aunt Hattie's to wish Press a happy birthday. The Colonel passed me and stopped until I caught up with him. "I suppose you're going to Press's." More statement than question. I nodded and climbed into his truck and settled back silently. He waited no more than half a minute before he spoke. "Son, no woman is worth the pain you're experiencing. You're going to have to let her go."

"I can't, Colonel. I don't want to breathe if I can't have her."

"I loved a young girl once. She lived here on this place

a long time ago. I was sixteen and she was seventeen. I don't know why I'm telling you this. I guess that I care for you and your brother and I don't want either of you to feel pain."

He was through talking. We pulled into Press's yard. Patty drove up behind us and blew the horn and waved. Press came to the front door and stepped out on the front porch. "Morning, Colonel. What no good are you two boys up to? Hattie Bell, come out and greet your guests."

Patty got out of our car and looked up at Press. "I'm ready to ride that horse now, Press." Press shook his head in dismay. "I've been practicing," Patty continued.

Press looked at us. "Colonel, will you and Matty excuse me a minute or two. This boy sure don't believe lard is greasy." He walked to the barn where he kept Magic and emerged in less than a minute with the horse saddled. "Take him to the garden spot before you get on, Patty." He directed my brother. "Hattie'll fuss at me if you break an arm."

"Where is Aunt Hattie?" I asked.

"She's upset because of some crazy dream she had last night."

I have to give Patty his due. He stayed on Magic for two seconds this time, but this time he went in the air higher so I guess that evens it up.

Magic calmed down after a few stiff-legged jumps,

then walked over and stood in front of the barn. Patty glared at the horse and swore under his breath. By the time he reached the spot where we stood he was smirking and I knew he had thought of some wise-ass remark. Before he could say anything we heard the shot of a high-powered rife echoing through the pine trees from the west. Press spoke first. He called loudly, "Hattie Bell, come serve our guests some coffee and pound cake while I go check on that rifle shot."

Aunt Hattie had stayed in the house since we arrived. This was totally unlike her. She was usually the perfect hostess when we stopped by. She came to the door and her eyes were wet. Her voice shook when she spoke. "Press, don't go. Please man don't go and leave me by myself. They's evil out there, Press." She didn't acknowledge anyone in the yard except her husband.

"I got to go, woman, it's my job, now you take care of our guests till I get back." He walked quickly to his horse and was riding toward the direction of the rifle shot before she could say anything more.

We sat on the porch in rocking chairs, and she cried silently. Ten minutes passed before it came, but she knew it was coming, of that I'm positive. She jerked her head toward the west even before the sound came. One single shot. The Colonel got up and excused himself. "I'll go see about Press, Aunt Hattie. Come on, Matty." Before we reached the truck the black riderless horse emerged from the woods a quarter-mile away. The horse stood at the edge of the trees and looked around bewildered. The animal would skitter for the barn then wheel around and trot back to the edge of the woods looking for his master.

Aunt Hattie looked through her tears and spoke in a quiet voice. "Colonel, will you and the boys go bring him home? I'll need to clean him up some."

On an unusually cold Saturday, seven days after Preston Leroy Angry died, two white boys, one on either side of the finest and most noble woman on earth, listened to the words of the hymn "Swing Low, Sweet Chariot," and Aunt Hattie and I and almost one hundred black mourners openly wept. Patty walked outside, but he didn't fool me.

The sheriff and two of his deputies spent weeks scouring the landscape of the plantation where Press's body was found looking for clues and finding none. They questioned Bunk Bartlet and all the other low-lifes that lived around the plantation or hung out at the Plantation Club. No one had heard or seen anything.

Press's black horse finally came back to his pen, but he stayed at the west end and stared toward the woods each day. No one ever put a hand on that horse again.

Nate pleaded with the Colonel for weeks to let him have his way. He was convinced and so was I that his knife could get more information than fifty deputies asking questions ever could, but the Colonel was adamant. After a time Nate lost patience. I heard him talking to the Colonel. "Colonel, I'm unwilling to wait on that stupid sheriff any longer. I'll find the man who killed Press and do it the way of my people."

"Nate, the only thing that separates us from them is that we are willing to abide by the law and the rules. You and I fought a great war against the same sort of people twenty-five years ago. They were the lawbreakers just as surely as these people we are confronting today are the lawbreakers. You are a soldier, and I expect you to behave like one."

"Are we to wait until the sheriff and his men give up before we do anything?"

"If nothing is uncovered before next week I will go to that beer joint and offer a reward of ten thousand dollars for information. I've never known these type people to remain loyal when money was at stake."

The Colonel had us drive him to the beer joint the next Saturday afternoon. He reasoned that if he caught the place full of people then someone might come forward immediately with incriminating evidence against the killer. Again I watched as he disappeared through the door and again I felt an emptiness. Patty felt just as apprehensive as I.

We knew that the Colonel would be mad if we went in to check on him, so we sat in the car and waited. A half hour elapsed and I was beginning to think he might be dead and that the people inside were afraid to come out and tell us. We heard the siren first. Moments later in the distance we could see a flashing red light, and in a moment an ambulance roared into the parking lot and to the front door of the beer joint.

In a trance, Patty and I walked toward the scene and watched in unbelieving horror as an old gentleman in his seventies was carried out the door on a gurney and placed in the ambulance, more dead than alive. With tires spinning, the ambulance headed for Albany with its siren blaring, and I led a zombie in shock to the car, opened the door, and put him in. With a rage that was totally uncharacteristic, I walked back and asked an old wino at the door what had happened. He said, "One of the boys shooting pool told that gang of thugs, leaning against that wall over yonder, who the old man was. One of 'em says, 'Let's show the gray-headed old bastard what poor folks do for entertainment, besides that, I ain't been in a fight in I can't remember when.' Well, one thing led to another after that."

I stepped through the door and looked at every man in the place. Some of them I had seen, some of them had been with Bunk the day they killed all the rabbits. Acid couldn't have etched a more vivid memory in my mind of what each of them looked like. I walked to the car and drove to the plantation, thinking that if I had my way, twenty-four piss-smelling bastards would be scratching their crotches in hell tomorrow morning.

CHAPTER 16

The Cattle of Bickerstaff

I STOPPED BY MR. BICKERSTAFF'S PLACE AND TOLD HIM WHAT had happened at the Plantation Club. I then asked if I could borrow some of his bulls for a while.

On his way to the door he said, "Take anything I've got." He left for the hospital. I drove to Nate's house, then Chief's, and recounted to them everything that happened and a lot that I'm not sure happened but it sounded good. When the sun hung low on the western horizon, we took the big cattle truck from Mr. Bickerstaff's barn to his bull pens and loaded eighteen very unhappy Brahma bulls. I assured everyone involved that I had obtained permission from Mr. Bickerstaff.

Patty had completely recovered from his state of shock and had returned to his former persona. "If this works, we're going to be in a shitload of trouble. You know that, don't you?"

Patty and Nate picked up the tack van from our plantation. They decided that even though what we were doing was my idea, it might well turn out to be worth immortalizing, so Patty collected the sixteen-millimeter camera and tripod. When he and Nate pulled into the parking lot of the Plantation Sportsman's Club he got out and, like a young Cecil B. Demille, positioned himself to produce and direct his first movie. Nate drove the eight-foot-high van to the rear of the club and backed up to the only rear door of the cinderblock building. Small, greased dogs could have gotten out the back door if they didn't have a beer belly. No one else could. Two nose pickers were on the side of the building relieving themselves as he came around the building toward the front and, with camera rolling from the distance, Nate lifted them both up by their necks and slapped their heads together, like any ordinary man might clap his hands. This was just in case they had anything to do with the Colonel.

The front of the building had one steel door and two windows with steel bars over them, and behind these were almost one hundred half-drunk rednecks and thugs belching and scratching their crotches.

Chief and I pulled into the parking lot and did a 180-degree turn. The big bulls were getting nervous and were becoming more agitated as we carefully backed over three motorcycles on the way to the front door, which was snatched open at the last minute by Nate. And I, little Matty, pulled the chain that let the gate up, and eighteen scared and excited bulls out. We were on our way to stardom.

Associated Press and United Press International picked up the story from the Albany television station on Sunday. On Monday, the twenty-second of April, I got to meet Walter Cronkite and Eric Sevareid. April 22nd was, also, according to Archbishop James Usher, the day the creation of the earth occurred. It took place at exactly 8:00 P.M. on April 22, 4004 B.C. The Irish cleric made his calculations in the midseventeenth century after studying the ages of the Old Testament patriarchs, long genealogies, and other biblical details. And on Monday, April 22, Patty's film (which they paid him for with an undisclosed amount of money, which he refused to share) was shown from coast to coast on the seven o'clock news. I was a hero in my own mind. I had knocked the winning run, I had caught the winning touchdown, I had saved the maiden from the dragon, I had pulled Superman's cape and unmasked the Lone Ranger. I thought how much the Colonel was going to appreciate what I had done. I told Patty. He exploded.

"What the Colonel is gonna do is kill us. If he finds out what we've done he's gonna throw a fucking fit. The only chance in hell we've got is to keep him from watching the news tonight. If that don't work, I'm going to tell him it was your idea."

"Let's tell him it was Nate's and Chief's idea," I pleaded. "He won't get as mad with them. I'll bet you he takes away our car if he thinks you thought this up."

"You aren't putting that monkey on my back, Matty. You thought of it and I'm going to tell him you did."

"Patty, when you talked to that television guy, you said it was your idea. If the Colonel sees that interview, he's going to see you admitting that you thought it up."

Patty and I timed our arrival so that we could be at the hospital and make sure the Colonel wasn't watching television when the news came on. He was in much better spirits and physical condition than we expected, and as if to substantiate his improvement, a few minutes before seven, he told me to cut the television to the evening news. When I protested that it might give him a headache or something, he replied, "Thank you for being concerned but I'm sure my head will be fine. My old body will take a little time to mend though, I suspect. I caught a couple of news teasers earlier about southwest Georgia and I want to see what Walter Cronkite thought was so funny. Have either of you got a clue?"

Glumly we looked at the floor. I finally answered, "No, sir, not a clue."

First came the interview with Patty and me, then the full film along with the narration. The first bull to make it out of the building came through the window, knocking the burglar bars several yards into the parking lot. A scared-looking man with long greasy hair came out next and Nate broke his jaw. All of the bulls made it past Nate and Chief without getting a broken nose or jaw, but I didn't see a single man that passed within their reach who got off easily. New doors opened up in places that were previously solid walls. When the cinderblock walls got too scattered and weak to hold the tin roof up and the last of the ton and a half Brahmas burst through the remaining walls, the Colonel spoke for the first time, and boy, was he ever mad.

"Who in hell is going to round up those bulls?" he shouted. "I'm not paying one red cent for those torn-up motorcycles. If I had needed help with that riffraff, I would have damned well asked for it. It's a miracle you didn't kill someone. It's a damned mystery why the four of you aren't in jail. What in hell were you thinking about? Don't you realize that you'll be kicked out of school for good if you get put in jail. Hunting guides or not, I'm not getting the first one of you out of jail."

There didn't seem to be any placating the Colonel, so we left. Patty drove straight to the little trailer where the owner of the pile of rubble, that had, just two days before, been the Plantation Sportsman's Club, lived. As usual when Patty did the crazy things he did, and this was a prime example, I followed behind with a sick feeling in the pit of my stomach.

A beer-bellied man with a four-day-old beard opened the door and recognized us. Instant outrage clouded his face, but before he had a chance to speak, Patty raised his hand to forestall any outburst, and said in a voice that almost scared me, "Mister, you've got five days, starting this fucking second, to get your business in order and disappear. Now, if any charges are pressed by anyone, against anybody, or if you ain't gone in five days, Pine Knoll Cemetery is going to get a new resident. And just in case you're wondering where the two black guys are, take a wild guess who's got the crosshairs of a rifle scope centered on your nose." Patty spun on his heel and started for the car, not looking back, and I did the same; the only difference being that my legs didn't feel like they were going to hold me up. On the way I heard a murmured but very distinct "You two sons of bitches are crazy, and I'm going to go, but not because you're running me off. I didn't want to live in this goddam place anyway."

Within three days all eighteen bulls were brought back to Mr. Bickerstaff's by grinning landowners. Mr. Bickerstaff said that if the Colonel wouldn't get us out of jail, he would.

On Thursday, the Colonel got out of the hospital and drove straight to our house. Patty and I went out to meet him, and before he could speak, Patty said, "Colonel, I ain't never said this to anybody but Matty, but I love you" and I said, "Colonel, I ain't never said this to anybody but Patty and Leighanne, but I love you, too," and then tears started coming out of that old man's eyes, and out of mine, and Patty had to walk around behind the car and stare off into the woods, but I knew that he was crying too.

For the next several weeks, whenever Nate, Patty, and I had any free time we rode the countryside. Nate broke the jaw of several men that I recognized as being in that beer joint that Saturday afternoon. The rest went to Arizona or some other foreign country looking for jobs.

CHAPTER 17

A Letter from Athens

JUNE 2, 1963, BECAME A REALITY, AND NOT JUST SOME far-off date on a calendar. Patty and I stood in line with twenty-six other students, wearing stupid-looking black gowns, waiting for an unearned and meaningless piece of paper, and wondering what we would do next.

At precisely the moment I was handed my diploma, my fate was being sealed in concrete by a letter written in Athens, Georgia, mailed the next morning, and opened seven days later.

The senior class had raised enough money through various fund-raising projects to take a class trip to Washington, D.C., after graduation. Our lone chaperone was a twenty-nine-year-old bachelor named Dudley

Temples. He had been our homeroom teacher and was also the high school basketball coach. As was customary, everyone called him Coach, with the exception of Patty, who called him Dudley.

The Colonel had gone to our graduation, and afterwards gave us five hundred dollars each with this admonishment: "If you men want to go to college, then keep the money and build on it, and if you get through the first year without any help from anyone, I'll see that you get to finish."

I thought I would do that. If I made good grades and got accepted to medical school, he might lend me the money to go there. I left all but one hundred dollars for our trip in my secret hiding place. I knew for sure that his sage advice had been wasted on Patty. In fact, I would have bet the hundred dollars I took with me that he wouldn't have lunch money on the trip back from Washington.

We boarded the train in Atlanta, and three hours later I crossed the Georgia state line for the first time. The railroad had reserved a private coach for us, with the vacant seats to be used only if the train filled up. It didn't, so we had plenty of room. I picked a seat by myself in the rear of the car and watched South Carolina go by. The clickety-clack of the wheels on the Southern Crescent had reduced most of my classmates to dozing, but to me, each beat seemed to be saying "Leighanne, Leighanne." I glanced up, and in the aisle stood a girl named Brenda Davis, startling me out of my reverie.

She smiled and said, "A penny for your thoughts. No, that's trite and stupid. Your thoughts are worth more than that. I'll trade you the best surprise of your life for what you're thinking."

I said, "Even for a penny you'd be overcharged; they're not worth it."

"Then I guess I'll give you the best surprise of your life for nothing."

Without asking, she sat down, and for the first time since I had known her, I thought about how very pretty she was. It's strange, but when you're totally in love with a girl, as I was with Leighanne, you don't really consider how pretty or appealing anyone else is.

I immediately felt guilty, even though I hadn't heard a single word from Leighanne since January 1, and even though I really believed she had succeeded in breaking our bond. Brenda, very shyly at first, and then with a conviction that made me know that this was the end of a long incubation period, asked me, "Matty, do you find me sexy and attractive?"

I felt my face turning red and my ears burning, but I managed to stammer, "You're very pretty Brenda, but . . ."

She interrupted, "Ever since we were sophomores,

I've batted my eyes and flirted, and always managed to be where you were, and hundreds of other things to make you notice me. When we get back from Washington, I'm leaving for school in Boston; otherwise I'd never have the nerve to tell you all this, but damn you, you're going to pay attention to me for the next six days. For as long as I've known you, I've thought you were beautiful, but now I think you are gorgeous, and guess what, little man? You're the one I've chosen to make my virgin deflowering voyage with."

I stammered and blushed and said something stupid like, "But Patty and I are identical twins."

She retorted, "No, hell, you're not. When you laugh, I hear bells tinkling, and birds, and brooks and nice things. When I hear Patty laugh, I feel a chill run down my spine." I figured I could be nice to her for the next few days, without compromising my commitment to Leighanne.

Halfway through Virginia, Brenda had told me everything from her bra size to how she got all wet between her legs when she thought about me.

Two hours from Washington, Coach Dudley stood up in the front of the car and shouted for our attention. "All right, people, listen up. These are the rules and the dos and don'ts and the daily itinerary and the sleeping arrangements at the Hotel Washington. Now don't make me ashamed of you and don't do anything you wouldn't do in front of your parents." After a fifteen-minute lecture he was recapping the daily itinerary. The second day, he explained, would be dedicated solely to the Smithsonian Institution.

Patty leaned up to the girl in front of him and whispered something in her ear. When she giggled convulsively, the coach, who was a little neurotic anyway, blushed, thinking she was laughing at him. In order to regain the upper hand, he focused his attention on her and almost shouted, "Miss Sheldon, would you mind sharing with the rest of the class what is so funny?"

She blushed and looked at the floor and murmured, "Nothing, Coach."

At this point, fully convinced that he was the brunt of the joke, he insisted, and she protested, and he demanded that she stand and share the joke with everyone.

She stood, and in a tone that reflected her obvious anger, said, "Patty told me that in the Museum of Natural History, they have the gangster John Dillinger's eighteen-inch dick in alcohol, and he said that if that were true, the man could have run a pretty close second to him."

When the laughter stopped, and the coach's face had returned from crimson to a blush red, he stammered, "Patty, I know that when you open your mouth, anything on earth will come out except the Lord's Prayer, but please, for the next few days, just keep your foul mouth shut and your opinions to yourself."

We had a block of fifteen rooms on the eighth floor at the Washington. Patty and I got the room next to Dudley's, which was in the center, separating seven boys' rooms on one side and seven girls' rooms on the other. At eight o'clock in the evening, Patty called room service and said, "This is Coach Dudley Temples in room 808. Send me up a couple of six-packs of your premium beer and charge it to my room." He left, saying he was going to visit Dudley. I showered, watched TV, and went to bed at ten o'clock.

At eleven o'clock I awoke to a knock on the door.

"It's Brenda, Matty. I need to talk to you."

I shouted through the closed door, hoping she would go away, "Brenda, I'm not dressed! Can't this wait until morning?"

"Matty, don't be a prude. Unlock the door. Leave the light off, and I'll wait until you get back under the covers before I come in." I did exactly that, and she came in, and untying the sash on her terrycloth robe, got under the covers with me, wearing nothing but the naturally erotic perfume of her body. The aroma traversed the distance from my olfactory nerves to my private parts with the speed of light. I started to protest, but her hand had already relocated my brain to a lower region of my body, and for the first time in 155 days I didn't pine for Leighanne for four whole hours.

Sometime before dawn she said, "Wow, I never thought my first time would be this good. Matty, you fool, why haven't we been doing this for years?" And then she was gone. The next night was a repetition of the first, except I "protesteth not as mightily."

When Patty came in at daylight the first night we were there, he was muttering, "You know, Matty, that dude Dudley ain't half bad." The second night he came in at five A.M. "Matty, I do believe I'm creating a monster in my own image. Boy, that Dudley is becoming one depraved bastard."

The next day we took a tour bus to the Washington Zoo, an experience that for me would be a further awakening to the lack of knowledge I had for the world and its flora and fauna. A monotone tour guide led us by Bengal tigers and African lions and impalas and gnus and gazelles and hundreds of other animals I had never heard of before.

I thought, "I sure hope the Colonel never comes to this place. He'd have us planting feed patches all over Africa."

When we reached the panda's special cage, the tour guide's monotone changed, and with a touch of pride in his voice, he explained that the zoo had a female panda. "Since there are only 173 pandas left on earth, the Chinese government has loaned us a male for two years with the hope that the two will mate."

Something pulled Patty's cord. "You mean to tell me that it's going to take two years of foreplay before he does anything? Hell, man, my Uncle Charlie could screw the bear if he had two years to get her in the mood. What that boy needs is some pointers from me and Dudley here. By God, we'd have that lady panda begging for more the first day." We all looked at Dudley. He was laughing, and I knew he had coached his last game. Patty had succeeded in creating depravity in his own image.

I looked at the male panda, and I swear he was looking at Patty as if he hated him. He sauntered over to the female panda, sniffed in the appropriate place, and was greeted by a throaty growl that clearly meant, "Not now, I've got a headache."

Washington had cast its magic on my brother. He had watched the politicians and lawyers in their chauffeur-driven Mercedes, Lincoln, or Cadillac cars and was hooked. On the train back to Georgia, Patty told me he knew now that he was put on this earth to be a politician. "Matty, I'm a natural, I already know how to lie and cheat and steal, so I won't have to be taught like those congressmen and lawyers already there. I already know how to get inside people's heads. Just watch Dudley if you don't believe it."

Peachtree Station in Atlanta was where we said our last goodbyes, hugging and promising to write or keep in touch. We made plans to do the same thing as a class in five years. We made the same sincere yet empty and never-fulfilled promises that every senior class since the beginning of time has made.

Brenda came up to me at the train station—no tears, no raised voice, no promises expected. "Matty, I love you, and I'll love you for a very long time. If you ever get tired of chasing a ghost, I'd like a chance. You were my first and it would suit me just fine for you to be my last."

"Brenda, I'm sorry. I can't."

"Matty, you know my grandfather owned the bank, and when he died he left a trust fund that will give me a million dollars when I'm twenty-one. And you know that all you'd have to do is crook your finger, and you could have me and the money."

Everyone knew she was rich, but all I could say was "I still can't."

"Do you think I could see a picture of the girl, without any clothes on, that you are so absolutely hung up on?"

"Why would you want to do that?" I puzzled.

"Because," she said, "I've never seen a million-dollar piece of ass, and I've always wanted to."

Patty and I gave Dudley a ride home. I sat in the back

and wondered why you love and want someone, but they don't want you, and you've got someone who loves and wants you, but you don't want them. Patty borrowed five dollars for lunch.

I was thinking that it would be nice for a change to be like Patty. Nothing seemed to touch him, and he certainly seemed to enjoy life much more than I. Our train to Georgia had left at eleven o'clock the night before, and as we were leaving the hotel for the short trip to the station, fifteen or twenty of the nation's leading economic indicators, dressed in minidresses with fishnet stockings and high heels, were there to bid Patty and his new friend Dudley their fondest farewells.

"Hey, Patty, don't forget to send me the fifty you owe me."

"Patty, I'll quit doing this if you'll take me home with you."

"Patty, I didn't know you had a twin. Hell, we'll all move to Georgia."

"Patty, tell the coach when he comes back to Washington to bring a hard dick with him."

"Hey, Patty, I swear to God I think I love you, but no kidding, send me the fifty you owe me."

We drove to south Georgia. If I was going to college, I would have to work hard this summer and save every penny. I didn't even know what you needed to do to get accepted. I planned to try and call Leighanne and ask her what I should do to get into the university. She might be so impressed with me that she would start back seeing me.

I was asleep when Patty drove into our yard that night. Uncle Charlie was up and waiting for us. He had fixed a nice meal, which was now cold, but we ate it anyway. He talked and laughed and asked us a hundred questions about our trip. I could tell that he missed us, but he would never say it. I asked him if I had gotten any mail. "Not that I know of. Course now I don't ever check the mailbox. Seems like all I ever get is bills. If I paid all them danged bills we got, I never would have any money."

Early the next morning I walked to the mailbox hopefully, as I had every morning since she left. This morning was different—there was a letter to me from Athens.

Dear Matthew,

I've met someone who fulfills the criteria I set for my future. His life epitomizes everything that I've ever dreamed of. I do not love him, but I will learn to. We will be married in August. I will miss you very much.

Leighanne

CHAPTER 18

Basic Training

AN EARLY MORNING DOWNPOUR, VERY RARE IN JUNE, THAT would finish maturing the corn crop on the plantation, had quit its hair-trigger temper but had left mud-splattered leaves and the smell of ozone in the air. I was thinking that normally this time of the year we got all of our rains from towering thunderclouds that emerged from the southwestern part of the state in the late afternoons, built from the moist winds of the Gulf of Mexico—a place the old-timers called "St. Peter's Mudhole." It was, indeed, an odd thing to think, after reading Leighanne's letter and throwing it in the rain-filled ditch.

It was 9:00 A.M., June 9, 1963. Sixteen hours after I read Leighanne's letter I had volunteered for the draft, gotten drunk for the first time in my life, cried, thrown up, threatened to beat Nate's ass with one hand tied behind my back, and cried again. The next morning, after trying to find the dog that crapped in my mouth while I was asleep, I told Patty I had joined the army and was supposed to report for induction at Fort Benning, Georgia, in exactly two weeks.

He went ber-fucking-serk, and when my head quit vibrating from his verbal tirade, I looked out and both he and our car were gone. When he came back later that day, he walked up with his hands on his hips and almost shouted, "I've known since we were born that you didn't have much sense, but this time, you little son of a bitch, you're going to get us killed. You know that crazy bastard in the White House is going after those North Vietnamese people, and they're going to send us to goddam Vietnam, don't you? Well, by God, I hope they do, and I hope they shoot you in the goddam head, because you ain't got nothing up there anyway."

I, very tenderly and softly, in order to keep my head from vibrating, because for the first time in my life I had a really bad hangover, told him, "Why don't you just stay here, Patty. You don't have to go."

"You fool, I can't let you get killed by yourself. Uncle Charlie would kill me."

We decided not to tell anyone we were leaving. I left Uncle Charlie a note saying that we had joined the army and would be back after basic training. We locked our car in the unused mule barn behind the skeet range and walked to find Nate to take us to town. Aunt Hattie was waiting by the road that led to the main house.

"Morning," I said.

Her eyes were wet and sad. "I don't want my babies going where you headed. Something bad's going to happen. I feel it in my bones." We hugged her and told her goodbye and she dabbed her eyes. "I wonder how she knows everything that ain't happened yet," Patty said as we continued our search for Nate.

That afternoon when we left, the chartered Trailways bus had fourteen young men on it. The smiling army recruiter had seen us on the bus and waved goodbye as we pulled away from the terminal. Patty was in better spirits than I had seen him since we joined. I had told him that for ten weeks, while we were in basic training, that his sex life would be nonexistent. He looked at me smugly as if he knew something that I didn't. I asked, "Just how do you figure you're going to get to see a girl? That recruiter said it would be at least a month before we got a day off."

"Uncle Charlie said that anywhere there was a crossroads with two houses on it you could usually find some woman willing to screw. You find the crossroads and leave the rest to me."

I had, years before, noticed that on warm spring days, dogs would lie around in the warm sunshine and gnats would fly around their rear ends. There wasn't a square inch at Fort Benning, Georgia, where there wasn't a gnat. I'm not insinuating that if Georgia was suddenly trans-mogrified into an animal of the canine persuasion, that the anal-expulsive location would be Muscogee County, Georgia. To quote the 1940s radio show, "The Shadow knows." The gnats know too.

Our company of recruits going through basic training had approximately two hundred men. I say "men" with reservations because late that first night there, after a day of being shorn of proud hair, outfitted in oversized clothes, given immunization shots covering 285 domestic and exotic diseases, and finally being assigned a barracks and bunk by alphabetical last name, I walked down the aisle between the bunks to the latrines, and I heard one hell of a lot more sobs than snores. The next day we were marched to the post exchange to buy the basic necessities for a footlocker inspection display, and for our own personal hygiene. This was Saturday.

That afternoon at sundown, Patty and I risked court-martial, treason charges, and possible execution in front of a firing squad, and traveled the same path and direction that General George Patton had traveled twenty-two years before, when he had parked his tanks on the bridge between the cotton mills leading from Columbus, Georgia, to Phenix City, Alabama, and with a bullhorn had told the police department to turn his men loose or risk being the first casualties of the then-undeclared World War II. Patty got laid; I moped and brooded, and we both evoked our personal deity, asking not to be caught sneaking into our barracks at 3:45 A.M.

Exactly one hour and fifteen minutes later we were awakened by a maniac blowing a bugle.

The recruit in the bunk next to mine sang out, accompanying the bugle summons of reveille, "There's a soldier in the grass, with a bullet up his ass, get it out, get it out, better get it out fast."

That afternoon Patty and I set the tone for our next several weeks. It was Sunday, the 176th day of my hell without Leighanne. It was free time, except one couldn't go anywhere away from the company area. We were showing several recruits the refined art of seven-card stud. Patty and I were 250 dollars ahead and we had 23 dollars of our own money in the game. I swear we weren't using any of the tricks Uncle Charlie had taught us, but the Neanderthal three-striped sergeant in charge of our barracks decided, since we had all the money, we had started

the game, we must have cheated, and that he should con-
fiscate the money, which is what he did. His first mistake
was taking the money, which Patty considered sacred
because it was to be spent on sex and beer. His second
mistake was picking us to make an example of in order to
establish fear in the other recruits. His third mistake was
calling Patty a dumb-ass white boy. I was beginning to
think there just might be an ever-so-slight possibility that
I had made a mistake in joining the army. It did, however,
give me something to hate almost as much as the bastard
that Leighanne was marrying. From that Sunday afternoon until he left, the Neanderthal with three stripes
waged a fierce and vengeful vendetta directed toward
Patty and me.

Uncle Charlie used to say, "If you give a man a badge
and gun, or stripes in the army, if he's got any son of a
bitch in him, it will rear its ugly head." He also said, that
to his knowledge, there were more sons of bitches per
square mile in Fort Benning than in any other place on
earth.

I did know one thing, and I was absolutely sure about
this. When the dude picked Patty as an adversary, he
picked one that totally outclassed him. This boy was dog-
meat. He was fooling with a pro.

Since Patty had gotten us the collar and cap insignia
that belied our lowly rank and distinguished us from the

other basic-training recruits, we rushed through the evening meals and walked out of our company area, putting on our new rank. We usually walked to the beer gardens or the NCO club and shot pool until about thirty minutes or so before lights-out at the barracks.

One night, fifteen minutes before lights-out, the sergeant was sitting on the steps smoking. When we walked past, he said, "You dickheads haven't been out of the company area, have you?"

I replied, "No, sergeant."

He asked, "Where you been then?"

Patty answered, "The captain said we could go see the chaplain anytime we needed to."

The next night we rounded the building at the same time, and the yellow-toothed bastard was there again.

"I reckon you're going to tell me you've been to see the chaplain again."

"Yes," Patty said. "You see, Matty has this problem, and the chaplain's been trying to help him overcome it. Matty thinks he might have some homo sapien tendencies, but I don't think so. I think it's just a severe case of excessive flatulence."

The sergeant said, "Hell, that ain't no news to me. I could look at him and tell he was a little queer." After that we came in from a different direction, and if he was on the steps we went to the other door.

The barracks we were assigned to was a basic pre–World War II building, long and narrow with a door in the center of one end, and a door on the side between the sleeping area and latrine. On the end having the centered door were two private rooms, one on either side of an eight-foot-wide aisle that extended down the middle of a large open room. Entering the building, the private room on the left was where the sergeant resided. Twelve two-man bunks were positioned on either side of the aisle. Our bunk was the one closest to the sergeant's private room. At the far end of the room a set of steps led down to the latrine, where eight of the forty-nine occupants could shower at one time. Another eight could shave simultaneously, and another eight usually sat and gave living and audible testimony to the rigors that G.I. food put on the human digestive tract.

If anybody had told him, I would have denied it, but I sure did miss Uncle Charlie's cooking.

After the second week of unabated harassment from Sergeant Yellow Teeth, Patty was ready to murder, and I knew that one man's Armageddon was close at hand.

We advanced to the section of basic training where weapon training was a daily event. Each recruit had been issued an M-16 rifle and had spent days carrying the thing from place to place. We had cleaned it dozens of times, done the manual of arms hundreds of times, marched with it, slept with it, eaten with it, and now it was time to learn to shoot the thing. As was the typical way of doing business in the army, the firing range was seven miles away and, the best way anyone in command could figure for us to get there each day was to march, to walk flat-footed fourteen miles a day when we could have ridden. The motor pool had hundreds of deuce-and-a-half trucks sitting there idle, but the best way was still to walk. We left each morning at six, wearing a helmet liner and a ten-pound steel helmet on top of it. Each man carried a poncho and a full canteen. We were allowed to carry our weapons strapped across our shoulders. We marched single-file, one file on each shoulder of the road.

"Damn and hell, Matty, why did you ever join the army?" He asked me that every morning and several times each day while we marched to the rifle range.

The drill instructors were all sergeants. They would walk on the smooth surface of the road and keep us quiet and evenly spaced as we marched. They all wore the Smokey Bear hats so that no one would mistake them for trainees. At the firing range an observation tower was centered behind the firing line. Forty waist-deep foxholes, with sandbags stacked four deep around them, were evenly spaced to the right and left of the tower. The drill instructors would walk behind the foxholes cursing and shouting instructions to the nervous trainees as they shot at man-sized silhouettes spaced every fifty meters from two hundred meters out to a maximum of six hundred meters. The targets were spring-loaded, and after they were knocked down, they could be set back up by pushing buttons in the control tower. The object was to knock down as many targets as you could with the five-round clip of ammunition you were issued.

"Ready on the right?" Pause. "Ready on the left?" Pause. "Ready on the firing line?" Pause. "Lock and load, one five-round clip. Fire." These were the typical instructions we heard from the loudspeaker each time it was our turn in the foxhole. Patty and I were on the far right end of the line of foxholes, and eighty rifles were being fired simultaneously.

Our sergeant was giving some recruit hell on the far side of the observation tower. "Cease fire, cease fire, cease fire, cease fire. Lay your weapons down on the sandbags and back away ten paces," the loudspeaker boomed. Slowly the firing stopped, and hesitantly each man did as he was instructed. I looked at the observation tower, then beyond it I saw our sergeant, now hatless, peering over one of the sandbag emplacements. Again the loudspeaker boomed, "All right, which one of you dickheads shot Sergeant Grey's hat off?" Complete silence. "The shot came from the right side of the tower. Each of you come to attention. Now! Move it, goddammit!" Again the loud-speaker boomed.

Five sergeants, one with a hole in his Smokey Bear hat, stopped in front of each trainee and cursed and questioned him until they were satisfied that that man hadn't fired the shot. After almost two hours of yelling the sergeants got to Patty. I would be next.

Our sergeant, still wide-eyed, told the other sergeants, "This is the mother I've been waiting to question. It's either him or his queer brother. I'd bet my ass and my paycheck it was one or the other."

A burly sergeant towered over Patty and breathed down toward his face. "Did you shoot the goddam hat off Sergeant Grey?" he screamed.

"It couldn't have been me or my brother," Patty replied calmly.

"How in the hell do you propose to convince us that you didn't shoot his hat off?"

"Because we're the best shots in the whole battalion. Neither one of us would have missed his head."

The sergeant looked around at Sergeant Grey before continuing. He screamed, "How in the hell do you convince me that you ain't lying?"

"You issued each of us five live rounds. Count the down targets in front of our firing lanes."

On the march back Patty muttered, "Damn it, I meant to part the bastard's hair crossways. This rifle's shooting a tad high."

"How did you do that?" I whispered.

"You can hit the next to last target high and the same bullet will hit the last target low. I've been waiting all week for you to hit all five of your targets."

Two days later the sergeant found a crude black voodoo doll, dressed in olive drab, sporting three small stripes, and with long pins stuck in it, under his bed. Under his pillow were two crossed bones. The following day the sergeant, noticeably upset, tried to conceal his uneasiness by doubling his harassment of Patty and me. The next night he awoke from a fitful sleep, turned on his reading lamp, and found on his nightstand the severed head of a very large black dog that had been hit by a car that afternoon in front of the PX. For the next five days, he slept with the overhead light on and his door locked. The sixth night, a tile was quietly lifted from his ceiling and a four-foot, eastern diamondback rattlesnake was dropped on his bed.

All I can figure is that the snake must have struck the loose folds of the sergeant's baggy underwear and gotten his fangs hung. The forward motion must have kept it from shaking loose, because when the sergeant ran past our bunk toward the other end of the barracks, the snake was almost horizontal.

Thank the Lord, the worst of the bad smell and the mess on the floor was at the far end of the barracks.

While everybody else's attention was glued to the far end of the barracks, Patty walked in the sergeant's room and got exactly 273 dollars out of his wallet.

Long before Patty got back to the main barracks area, the sergeant had rounded the last bunk and cleared the steps at the side entrance, jolting the snake loose when he hit the ground at full speed.

The entire platoon was still staring open-mouthed at the door the sergeant had last gone through. Patty walked to that end of the barracks, dodging the sergeant's mishap, and cleared his throat. "Each of you has just experienced a strange phenomenon. You all had the same dream. If anyone thinks what he dreamed was real, then now is the time to say so."

Later that night a second lieutenant from Martin Army Hospital came to our barracks and almost apologetically asked if anyone had seen anything strange that night.

Our next sergeant was mean as hell, but he was fair. He was mean as hell to all of us.

On Saturday, August 17, at 1:45 P.M., something, I suppose it was the instincts that dated to my Indian ances-tors, maybe it was the red wolf, caused the hair on the back of my neck to rise. Without speaking and without really knowing why, I got off my bunk and walked the quarter mile to the forest ranger tower. I climbed to the top, and I don't understand why but I looked toward Atlanta, and a howl came from my throat that sounded like a lone red wolf on a cold Carolina night, and I knew without a doubt that at that very second she lifted the white veil from her face and looked south. I retraced my steps to the ground and sat at the base of the tower. Patty walked up and sat next to me with his arm around my shoulder until I quit shaking.

CHAPTER 19

Long Bien

NOVEMBER 1963 ARRIVED AT FORT JACKSON, SOUTH
Carolina, much the same as in south Georgia. The
dog fennel was blooming and led to fits of sneez-
ing. The goldenrod was the same golden color. The trees
wore their finest dress of showy reds and yellows then
slowly did a sad burlesque and waited for the pall of winter. No live oak trees spread their limbs and blessed the
land.

Patty and I were in our fourth week of infantry training school after finishing basic training, and he ranted,
"The only damn thing they're teaching us is how to walk
and run and I already know how to do both."

Three weeks later, the 325th day since Leighanne, the
shot of a high-powered rifle from a Dallas schoolbook

depository changed history. I shed tears with two hundred million other people. Patty said, "You just wait until that thief from Texas moves into the White House and see how many body bags they send to Vietnam."

The "thief from Texas" was sworn in as president exactly ninety-nine minutes after the charismatic victim received last rites. The next week he moved into 1600 Pennsylvania Avenue, and before it was over, 47,752 body bags were filled.

We ate Christmas dinner in a near-vacant mess hall in Fort Campbell, Kentucky. I, with a much-handled Christmas card postmarked Atlanta ten days earlier, on which was a single "I love you, Matty" written in pencil, and Patty, with a stack of ten-page letters from the ex-prostitute in Washington to whom he owed fifty dollars. It seems that after he left, she decided she was in love with him. She had changed jobs and was then working for a senator. Patty said, "She went from being a whore to working for a whore."

Two days after Christmas we received orders that would govern our lives for at least the next thirteen months, and for the next two days we reviewed training films on Southeast Asia. On the anniversary of "Leighanne and Counting," I left the continental United States for the first time, 33,000 feet in the air, headed for Vietnam. Since war wasn't declared on North Vietnam until August 4 of that year, we were sent as advisors to demonstrate to the South Vietnamese soldiers how to kill the Vietcong.

After Lyndon lied to America on national television, and told everyone that U.S. ships had been attacked by the North Vietnamese, Congress ratified his declaration of war. Patty remarked, "Thank goodness, we can kill those little geeks all legal-like now."

The U.S. Army had a buddy system at the time we joined. The system guaranteed that we would be stationed at the same army base through our tour of duty; otherwise I'm sure they would have separated Patty and me and sent him to Southeast Vietnam to get killed and me to Southwest Vietnam to get killed.

In a lot of ways, Vietnam was not that bad. The food was better than Uncle Charlie's, and the times that Patty badgered some tired gunnery sergeant into letting us fly as door gunners on the Huey or Chinook helicopters were kind of fun. We flew over swampy areas, and when the ducks spooked, Patty would go duck hunting with a .30-caliber machine gun. Each time he'd say, "Man, Nate would have an orgasm if he could be doing this." Patty had bought a New York City phone book to sit on when we flew in the copters. He had a paranoia about getting his genitalia shot off. He had field-tested the directory at two hundred yards with an M-16 rifle. When the projectile only reached the M's, Patty was satisfied his dick was safe.

We were stationed at Long Bien Army Base, South Vietnam, and within a very short time, I had divided the people I would be fighting with into two basic groups: those who were having problems handling the war and those who were not. I subdivided the former into (A) those having problems but still in control and (B) those having problems and depending on drugs or alcohol to help them cope. Then I subdivided the group not having problems into (A) those treating the war like it was a problem that needed all of their judgment and skill and (B) those who didn't have a problem with the atrocities of war; they just didn't care. I assigned each individual a category, and when I went on patrol I tried to get with as many "NHP-A's" as possible.

Patty and I tried marijuana for the first time, which was the last time for me but I'm not sure about him. We were on patrol somewhere south of the Mekong Delta, and a survey lance helicopter radioed that the area of elephant grass directly in front of us had an open area in the middle, and what appeared to be enemy activity. I was point man in our squad, and Patty was directly behind. As we slowly worked our way through the thick, razor-like, fifteen-foot-high grass, a bevy of very loud European jackdaws flushed directly in front of me. Patty was one second faster than I in reacting, and the instant he knocked me to the ground, the guns behind us killed about a half acre of very dangerous enemy cane. It scared me so bad that I almost lost control of my sphincter muscle. When I felt my pants and decided that I hadn't done anything childish I rolled over and emptied my rifle over the heads of the men behind me. To a man they hit the ground and I told them, "Just checking out your sphincter muscle."

When we reached the opening, the people who had been there were probably halfway to Cambodia, but they had left behind evidence of what they had been doing. The little field had been planted in marijuana, which had been harvested, then hung upside down to cure. We had interrupted them as they were stripping the cured leaves and putting them into the plastic bags scattered around every American base over here. Our mind-sets being that we were pretty sure we were going to get killed anyway must have tilted the scales in the wrong direction, because when a zit-faced kid pulled out a book of papers and passed the paraphernalia around, Patty and I both said, "Much obliged." Four or five "much obligeds" and several hours later, I awoke with the rising sun, and a deep conviction that a family of Vietnamese had crapped in my mouth while I was asleep.

An Asian honey guide was circling and squawking

overhead, obviously in an altercation with one of its more pugnacious neighbors. These birds would spend hours arguing with their neighbors about property rights and boundaries.

"A hungry fox saw some fine bunches of grapes hanging from a vine that was trained along a high trellis, and did his best to reach them by jumping as high as he could into the air, but it was all in vain, for they were just out of his reach, so he gave up trying, and walked away with an air of dignity and unconcern, remarking, 'I thought those grapes were ripe, but I see now they are quite sour.'" A Phrygian slave named Aesop wrote that fable in the sixth century B.C., and I wished like hell I could emulate that fox.

March 1 marked one year and two months since I had seen Leighanne. This was also the day we were given four days off and a ride to Saigon on the base hospital bus, along with fourteen female nurses. These nurses were rotated in shifts of ten days on duty and four days off. This system worked extremely well and kept burnout at a minimum. The nurses had reservations at the best hotel in Saigon and suggested we stay there also, which we agreed to do. On the way Patty quietly announced, "I'm going to screw the little blond in the third seat first. She's my kind of woman. I put my ear up to hers and could feel the wind blowing through. Yessir, give me tits over brains any day of the week."

We checked into the plushest hotel I had ever stayed in or had ever seen. The center of the hotel was a giant atrium. Glass-covered and climate-controlled, it was a tropical garden overflowing with orchids, flamboyant trees, and hibiscus. Brightly colored tropical birds flitted and squawked. A swimming pool was in the center of this manmade ecosystem.

I lay on my bed looking at the ceiling and thinking, "She's a black widow spider, an arachnid with a red hourglass on her belly. She used me to fulfill a need then sucked my body juices."

Patty was staring out the window, "judging the meat" and talking incessantly. When I didn't readily answer his staccato questions, he walked over and sat on his bed, and in the most serious tone I'd ever heard from him, he said, "Matty, I realize that if you had wanted me to know anything about you and Leighanne, or how you felt about her, you would have told me. You have told me, in different ways, and I've followed your ups and downs with her since we were thirteen. Matty, the fat lady has already sung; you just weren't listening. I think that you've given her your youth, and you don't owe her your manhood, too. Hell, man, she just broke your heart, she didn't castrate you. Now, get off your ass and listen to this plan I've got. There are fourteen nurses here, and only four nights, and I know I'm not Sir Isaac Newton, but I figure, if my math is right, that we get two each the first three nights and one the last. You stay in our room and set the clock for one o'clock, then you tell whichever girl's here that I'll be home in fifteen minutes and send her back to her room. I'll send another one at two o'clock."

I wouldn't have thought in my wildest dreams that it would happen that way, but by the third morning I was ten pounds lighter and eating a big steak for breakfast.

I suppose being involved in the daily commerce of waging war, or nursing and tending to the bloody results of that commerce, made a man and a woman thrown together for a moment in time grasp at the most temporary of strong emotions and momentarily think it to be love.

Andrea told me on Friday, "You know, Matty, I thought I knew what I was doing over here, but I don't. I know that I don't want to mend wounds, violently inflicted, ever again. I think that this, making love to you, is what I want to do most."

Each one had a reason; each one had a story, each a most-loved song, a boyfriend or husband back home, a family and a best friend. And each of us lived our lives in quiet desperation until fresh-made love took the edge off a reluctance to tell, and we talked.

Debbie told me she liked men and tolerated their groping and probing but explained, "I much prefer oral sex with a man who is very gentle. In fact, I think I would even prefer a gentle female over a groping man."

And exhausted and almost asleep on Saturday morning, Jo told me, "I use men. I hate men, but I need men for a sexual gratification I can't fulfill by myself. If I could, I wouldn't give a damn if a dick-eating virus was introduced to the drinking water of every city in America. Matty, can we pretty please do that again?"

It was Sunday morning, and we had to catch the bus back to Long Bien the next morning. A dull ache reminded me that Leighanne wasn't coming back to me, but today was here, and the morning was beautiful, and there was one more nurse. Patty had suggested a party the night before, and after receiving everyone's enthusiastic approval, he ordered three kegs of beer and had them set up at the pool. He hired a bartender, and instructed him not to let any girl's glass run dry. He hired a four-piece American band to play until his money ran out.

An uneasy feeling was playing around my lower abdomen because I didn't think Patty had enough money to settle his bill the next morning, and I didn't want to face the embarrassment that usually accompanied this feeling. I intended to ask him when I next saw him.

I sat in the atrium section of the dining room, eating a steak with eggs for breakfast, when he bounced in. He sat down, taking the American newspaper I was reading out of my hand as he did, and when the maitre d' came over, he ordered a dozen oysters on the half shell and a poached salmon. The waiter asked him to repeat the order, explaining that in sixteen years he had never taken a breakfast order like this one. Very patiently, Patty explained. "Look man, it's a well-known and documented fact that oysters increase a man's sexual potency." He looked at the expressionless man and said, "Look junior, oysters make you want to fuck and fish are the best brain food available, and I'm going to need an awful lot of both those things today."

When the waiter walked away, muttering that he'd be glad when the North Vietnamese took over the city, Patty announced, "Matty, I'm going to have myself an orgy tonight that's going to make what those Roman guys who wore those short skirts did seem like a slumber party."

"Patty, you were born with basically the same equipment as me. If you're going to lie, tell it to somebody who doesn't know any better."

Unable to think of an argument against my point, he sidetracked, "Matty, you remember the story about John Henry, the steel-driving man?" He quoted, "'I'm John Henry from the Black River country where the sun don't never shine. I ain't the best spike driver in the world, but the man what was is dead and that don't leave nobody but me.' I'm the same way about fucking, the best there was is dead and that don't leave nobody but me."

I interrupted, "Patty, do you have enough money to cover your bill when we check out?"

He acted as if he didn't hear me and continued, "Matty, can you imagine someone like King Solomon? He had 740 wives and 360 concubines, and he gave them all up for one woman. Boy, not me. She was the Queen of Sheba, and he called her the Rose of Sharon, the Lily of the Valley, the Queen of the Nile, and her name was Nefertiti. Matty, have you ever let a goat eat corn from the palm of your hand? Boy, that lady must have felt like that goat nibbling out of your hand."

He said just to wait and see about the orgy he was going to have, but not to wait in the pool after the first hour, because the pee would burn my eyes.

"Patty, you're full of crap. Just because you do something doesn't mean everybody else does the same thing. Do you have enough money to cover your bill?"

He answered, "If I can prove to you that all fourteen of those women pee in the swimming pool, then you pay for the party and the hotel bill. If they don't, I pay for the party, and our room, and I give you next month's pay."

I wasn't a genius by any means, but Patty had just made the worst bet I'd ever heard. He was going to be one broke fool in the morning. I took him up on his bet then I asked him again, "Patty, are you sure you've got the money to pay for all this?"

He reached over and patted my leg and said, "Don't worry, little brother, I've got the bill taken care of."

I should have known better. He went down to the hotel apothecary and told the pharmacist he had a kidney infection and had taken some medicine one time before. He swore that he couldn't remember the name of those pills, but he did recall that they turned your urine red. When the eleventh red cloud came to the surface of the pool that afternoon as the woman frantically waved her hands under water, I asked Patty if he'd like to back out of the bet. Several hours later I had this sick feeling in the bottom of my stomach as I counted money into the band leader's hand.

The next morning, at the registration counter, I took the only-to-be-used-in-case-of-a-heart-attack money from behind the secret flap in my wallet, emptied all my pockets, and was still twenty dollars short. Patty came by and loaned me the twenty and said not to be in any hurry to pay him back; he had two more where that one came from.

"Just how in hell did you plan to pay the bill if you had lost?"

He just shrugged and walked off saying he was going

to find that waiter and get a refund. One of the oysters he ate yesterday morning was a blank; only eleven of them worked.

Uncle Charlie had told me on numerous occasions, "Matty, when you call a bet your brother has made, it's like pissing in your britches to stay warm. You feel good for a few minutes, then you realize that you've made a terrible mistake."

On the hospital bus going back to Long Bien, one of the nurses said, "You know, Matty, you've got the strangest brother. He told all of us yesterday morning that we either had to lend him a hundred dollars each, or pee in the pool, one or the other. Reckon why he would want us to do that?"

Sometimes I hated that little son of a bitch.

CHAPTER 20

Revelation

ONE GOOD THING HAPPENED ON THIS PARTICULAR TOUR OF duty. It didn't start well at all, but it turned out surprisingly well. A young private first-class from Augusta, Georgia, obviously faced with some pretty ominous personal demons, was trying to exorcise them with cocaine. Every time we saw this kid, he was so high that a midair collision was a good possibility. I believe that probably half the military in Vietnam were doing drugs, mostly marijuana.

Some, like Joe from Augusta, were in pretty deep, though, and as long as they did it without any reckless endangerment to anyone else, I could live with their stupidity. One day on patrol our eleven-man squad stopped long enough to eat a lunch of Uncle Sam's gourmet recipe chicken, packed in a tin can. As was his customary way, Patty squatted, sitting on his helmet liner. Joe's hands shook like leaves on an aspen in high wind, and the tell-tale signs of a twitching mouth and a muscle tic indicated that the cocaine had run out before Joe's next payday.

Joe's stomach was cramping from withdrawal, and when he backed up to a tree and attempted to slide to a sitting position, the trigger on his rifle got hung on a limb and he accidentally discharged his weapon, shooting the helmet liner out from under Patty. A piece of the shattered plastic liner cut a blood vessel on the foreskin of Patty's penis, and I'm here to claim witness to the fact that it scared the walk-about dog crap out of him. When he looked down and saw blood, he started screaming, "Matty, my dick's gone! Matty, don't you let a soul try to save me! I want to bleed to death! Oh Lord, what am I going to do? Matty, I want you to kill that goddam dope-head! Oh Lord, why didn't you let that stupid bastard shoot my leg off instead? Matty, I want you to call Oral Roberts and Billy Graham and ask them to pray for my dick."

The next day, after Patty had calmed down and ascertained that his reason for strutting was intact, he and I went to find "private first-class soon to be ex-drug user." Patty put his arm around the boy's shoulder and, like a father speaking to his young son, said, "Now, Joe, Matty here is going to be the odd man, and I'm going to be the even man, and what this means is that on the odd days Matty's going to beat your ass, and on the even days I'm going to beat your ass until you decide that you're going to stop using that crap you're using."

Eleven days after being given this ultimatum, Joe quit cold turkey. I never would have thought that we would get thanked for beating a person's ass. Strange world.

■ ■ ■

THE END OF OUR FIRST YEAR IN THE ARMY WAS PUNCTUATED BY a two-week R-and-R leave. I caught an air force cargo plane to San Diego and a commercial jet from there to Atlanta and on to Albany. Patty caught a plane to Hawaii. This was to be the first time, other than last Christmas, that we had spent more than a couple of days apart since birth, and I had strong reservations about Patty's ability to stay out of trouble. My worries proved to be unfounded. Other than a little trouble he had at the priciest bar in Honolulu the first night there, he was a perfect gentleman. It seems he spent the other thirteen days of his leave sleeping all day and playing gin rummy all night with the night jailer of the Honolulu police department. The police were even nice enough to drive him to the airport his last day and see him off to Saigon.

My intentions when I left Vietnam were to fly to

Albany and go directly to the plantation. The last letter I had gotten from the Colonel was vague but alluded to the fact that he was experiencing some medical complications. Evidently, he had taken a leave of absence as CEO from his company and was staying on the plantation until he got better. This bothered me a great deal, and I wanted to see for myself that he was okay. The circumstances reminded me too much of something Chief had told me when I was a small boy. I asked him what happened to the dogs when they got too old to hunt.

"When a dog gets too old, I don't pen him up anymore. He knows when it's time to die, so he goes off to his favorite place and just waits."

She never told me how she knew I was coming home, but when the Southern Airlines commuter landed and I collected my luggage and started for the counter of the rental car agency, she was there. She had been drinking, but not much, and she was slouched to one side, a mink coat draped over one shoulder, and before I could say anything, she said, "Matty, you bastard, I cannot finish. I do not know what you have done to me , but I can't have an orgasm. I have the most perfect husband and the most perfect life and the most perfect everything, but I feel like a whore when he touches me, and I don't know what to do." By this time she was crying, and I felt like I had a cocklebur stuck in my throat. I didn't make it to the plantation that day or the next, and we proved that her inability to have an orgasm wasn't a permanent thing. On our third day together she admitted in a small, quiet voice that she had to go back to Atlanta. I said she had damned well best make up her mind what she wanted, because I fully intended to go back to Vietnam and fuck myself into a coma if she didn't tell me the truth about how she felt.

"Have you not made love to another woman, Matty?"

I stole the answer from Patty. "You broke my heart, Leighanne, you didn't castrate me."

"I hate you, Matty. Why don't you just leave me alone? No, I've been lying to myself. I adore you; I love you. I have loved you since you were twelve years old. When I'm with you, I think I can fly; I feel like singing. But I have a husband and a new life and responsibilities, and I guess our stars were crossed. I guess you and I were not meant to be."

I have no idea what slept in my mouth that night while I was passed out, but I sure would hate to meet up with it on a dark night.

The next morning after I had thrown up, hopefully for the last time, I drove to the plantation and found out that the Colonel would be at Emory University Hospital for a couple of days undergoing treatment. I cornered Aunt Hattie, and she finally told me that the Colonel had cancer but had assured everyone that he could lick the thing.

I spent the next two days visiting Uncle Charlie, Nate, and Chief.

One day when they were busy I visited the graves of my mother and father behind Macedonia. The lot was large enough for several more graves, and I thought that one day, me, Patty, and Uncle Charlie would fill part of the space. Her headstone posted her date of death, and his was two months later: Elizabeth Katherine and Augustus Marcellus. Two people I had never known. I always knew somehow that he had planned his own death because he missed her so much and blamed us for her death. I touched the grave of the mother I'd never seen, and I knew that if she had lived she would have loved and wanted me and Patty.

I had grown a mustache and my face was fuller. I had also gained several pounds in the year that I had been gone. I guess killing people had taken the boyish look from my face. I'm sure that my looks had changed a great deal, for whatever reason. When the Colonel returned to the main house, I was waiting for him. He looked long and hard before he smiled, and with his old lively step, he met me halfway, where we shook hands, then hugged. We had dinner together that night, and the Colonel intermittently talked and stared at me. Afterwards, we sat in the library with a brandy and talked. He finally excused himself, returning with an old picture album. He handed it to me and instructed, "Look at this, Matty, and look close. You and I may have a long night ahead of us."

The front pages were filled with old black and white pictures of people I didn't recognize and places I couldn't readily discern. I turned the pages wondering why the Colonel had asked me to look at pictures that meant nothing to me, and as I focused my attention on the next page, I stared at a picture of myself. An old black and white photograph of a young man with short hair and a mustache, framed in a yellowed border and cracked with age or handling, filled the page. I looked at the picture, and looked up at the Colonel, and he was staring at me, trying to gather from my expression whether I understood more than he about what this photograph meant.

He spoke first, "I think you know what's going on. Now, I might be old, and I might be sick, but something's going on, and you had damned well better tell me."

I felt a lump in my throat and I could feel my eyes beginning to mist. I managed to say, "You're my grandfather. You're my father's real father."

He got up and walked to the window, staring out, studying the moon or the dark live oaks, or maybe nothing at all. A full five minutes passed as he tried to sort out his thoughts and turned the pages of his mind. He turned to face me, and his hands shook slightly. His eyes were beginning to brim with tears, and I knew that in that very brief time he had lived his youth again. He had swept the cobwebs from the darkest closets of mind, and he had remembered. When he finally spoke, the tears were running freely down his face, and he said, "Why didn't somebody tell me so that I could enjoy my family while I was alive and healthy, instead of having to wait until I'm dying!"

CHAPTER 21

News from Home

IF WE LIVED TWELVE MORE MONTHS THROUGH THIS GROSS stupidity they call a war and made it home with all our limbs, I wondered what Patty and I would do to make a living. I was thinking these thoughts exactly one week after the Colonel told me he was dying. I was also up to my chin in a rice paddy that smelled of human excrement, trying to look exactly like a clump of rice, so the Vietcong soldiers walking across the far levee wouldn't see me. If we got caught, I would never hear the end of it. Every time we went on patrol Patty got a hollow bamboo about twelve inches long and stuck it in his back pocket, and on several occasions he insisted I needed to do the same. And there he was five feet from me and perfectly concealed, under water, breathing through that hollow reed. They went by without seeing us, though, and I pulled Patty up. The first thing he said was, "I wonder what we're going to do for a job when we get back and the Colonel's dead."

"How did you know . . . ?"

He interrupted, "You didn't directly say it. I knew something was wrong when you put that picture of him and me and you by your bed." It was quiet for a few seconds as I waited for him to explain. "When I was in jail in Honolulu, I called the plantation and talked to Aunt Hattie. She told me she saw you crying after you and the Colonel had dinner the night he came home from the hospital."

I sat silently, not trusting my voice.

"Did you tell the Colonel we are his grandsons?"

"I didn't think you believed that he was our grandfather."

"Matty, I knew about it for years before you found out. I knew that you would tell him if I ever let you know I believed it too."

"I probably would have."

"What did he say when you told him?"

"He said that we should have told him long ago when we first knew. He said he howled like a wolf sometimes too. And he didn't know why."

I hated the Vietcong almost as much as I hated Leighanne's husband, and I hated him almost as much as I hated the stupid bastards in Washington who were underwriting this mass murder.

Two months had passed since I got back from Georgia. Ten more and we'd be home for good. The letter was plain, just my name and APO, no return address, but I knew with every nerve in my body that she had written it.

Dear Matthew,

You have completely ruined my life, and I never want to see you again. When I left Albany and came back to Atlanta, I felt that I would die if he tried to touch me, so I told my husband that I had some female problems, and that it would be perfectly all right, as far as I was concerned, for him to find a mistress until I could get my problem resolved. He picked a nineteen-year-old student nurse. We were divorced yesterday. They were married today. I have told my family that under no circumstances are they to give my address or phone number to anyone.

Leighanne Carter

The war dragged on and on. Time seemed to be stuck in the muck and mire. It seemed as if we should be going forward and making time pass, but then I'd look at a calendar, and no time had passed. I asked Patty how many people he thought he had personally killed, and with a resoluteness that told me he was no longer a mischievous boy, he said, "With my rifle or knife I've killed twenty-three and wounded seven; riding as door gunner in the copters with a machine gun, somewhere between forty and fifty, and I don't know about dropping stuff in the tunnels." I really looked at Patty and saw him for the first time in a long time. I saw him for what he had turned into. There was a little gray in his hair that wasn't there before, and I saw that he didn't laugh as easily as he once did. I hated every goddam politician in Washington for doing this to my brother.

Sixty days, and it would be over and we could go home. Patty and I received the letter from Uncle Charlie.

Dear Patrick and Matthew,

The Colonel died last week. They buried him at sea on Sunday. His last few weeks he instructed everyone not to contact either of you concerning his condition, and before he died he left instructions that you not be told until after the funeral. Yesterday a lawyer came by the house, and it seems the Colonel has left to me the house we live in and two hundred acres of land. He also left me a good deal more money than I will ever need. The lawyer said that the Colonel left the balance of the plantation to the two of you. I talked it over with Chief and Nate and we figured that you'd need us, so we're staying.

Yours truly,
Charles Robert E. Lee Anderson

We read the letter together, and I felt like crying, but the past two years had destroyed my ability to show that kind of emotion again.

Patty asked, "Matty, do you know what Valhalla is?"

"No."

"It's where the Colonel is. It's the great hall of immortality where all valiant warriors are received by Odin."

I said, "Did you know that was his name? Do you know that it never occurred to me to find out what our uncle's name was? Hell, I thought Charlie was the only name he had."

"Me, too."

The next day it came, a nine-by-twelve manila envelope with the return address: Ivy and Burns, Attorneys at Law. Again, we opened the letter together. A cover letter from the lawyer explained that he represented the Colonel and had been instructed to send the enclosed and sealed document to us only after the Colonel's death.

My Dear Grandsons,

How I envy your courage and fortitude. You are in a war that is unneeded and obviously unwanted by the American people. Yet you stay and fight, ever uncomplaining, for the rights and freedoms of a country that is completely alien and unfriendly toward you. I am indeed proud to be able to claim that my humble blood flows through your noble veins. I have left the plantation, which God loaned me for my lifetime, in your care. I can only remind you, as I often did when you were small children, that you are the stewards of the land and it now falls your duty to leave it in better condition than you found it. In the third chapter of Ecclesiastes of God's Holy Word, the son of David said, "To every thing there is a season, and a time to every purpose under heaven." I have fulfilled twenty-seven of those purposes that he spoke of, and now there is only one left to do. It is time for me to die. I only hope that I can be as brave as you men. I have given Nate my last order. He is a good soldier, and when the pain gets unbearable for me, he will carry it out. I'm only afraid that he is far more distraught than I know, so see after him when you come home. I remember once at the crossroads when the two of you told me that you loved me. This is my first time saying it, also, but I love you, too.

Your Grandfather

Patty walked off and stayed gone all day. When he came back he said, "I wish I had gone with you when you told him."

CHAPTER 22

Homecoming

TWO MONTHS LATER PATTY, ME, AND A HALF-DOZEN OTHER soldiers stood in our dress uniforms on the muster field at our base. We were there to be recognized in a ceremony that turned my stomach. They saluted us and honored us and put medals on us for killing a bunch of scared little guys. Had the world gone crazy? These people, who spoke their prepared speeches and put medals around our necks for breaking a commandment, were the same people who had worshiped the Lord and his Ten Commandments the day before.

At the end of the ceremony, a bored journalist from California asked us for any comment we might have, and in the most eloquent manner that I had ever witnessed, Patty answered, "In the late 1800s, a small tribe of Nez

Perce Indians, led by a wise man named Chief Joseph eluded the U.S. Cavalry for almost two years. When the cavalry finally caught them in Canada and forced the chief to take an oath not to fight the army again, he said, 'I will fight forever, no more.' Now, you can quote me, James Patrick MacDonald, as saying, "I will fight no more, forever.'"

Anyway, in two weeks it would be over for Patty and me. We could join the VFW if we wanted to. Patty told me that since our future had been pretty well assured, he wanted me to know that he didn't have a thing against me, but that he had made a few decisions. "I'm going to live in the guest house down by the lake so I don't disturb you at night." He paused. "Matty, do you remember the time when Shithead was visiting, and we asked Uncle Charlie if we could go to the lake with Nate? He told us that he didn't want us to go near any water until we learned how to swim. Boy, that old bastard's a hoot, ain't he?" He shook his head and smiled. I couldn't believe it, but Patty was actually thinking fondly of Uncle Charlie.

He continued, "Now, I know you've got a better business head than I do, so you do the thinking, and I'm going to learn to sing bass so I can help out with the fucking at all the funerals." I said okay, and he continued, "I'm going to stay in Hawaii for a few days when we get out, and I might hire a couple of those slant-eyed women to come work for us." He said that some of the folks the Colonel had working on the plantation were old enough to have personally listened to Lincoln's Emancipation Proclamation on the radio, and he'd be damned if he was going to be nursing somebody who was supposed to be waiting on him. He added, "Matty, when I leave here, I think I may stop by Washington and bring that girl home with me. I've never been in love before."

"Take my advice and don't do that. That love crap won't do anything but make you miserable. Now that I'm over Leighanne I never intend to fall in love again. No sirree, not me, I mean not ever again. I am through with women."

"What the hell you going to do about sex?"

"I don't know. The only thing I know for sure is, since I got over her, I'm not ever going through that again."

"When I get back to Georgia, I'll fix you up with that tall girl named Diane. You know, the one who graduated from high school with us."

"Patty, I don't need any help with that. Besides she's slept with every single boy that ever went to our high school except me."

"Good God from Zion, Matty, you act like the girl was promiscuous. The school wasn't that fuckin' big."

We spent our last few days on the base getting ready to muster out. In five days we would be on our way home to a life that would be far different from the life we had led when we simply worked on the plantation. After lunch Patty wandered up from the mess hall and found me. He said, "Matty, let's go out one more time with the choppers. It'll be the last time either of us'll ever see this place."

I didn't want to go. I felt a nagging that I couldn't explain. The nagging grew to near panic as I looked at my brother and something was missing.

I said, "Patty, let's leave these guys alone. The war's over for us. Please man, let's leave it like that."

He smiled gently as if he knew something I didn't. "Stay here then. I simply want to see the country one time without a rifle in my hand."

"Patty, something's wrong. Let's don't go."

"We've already crossed the Rubicon. Pompey isn't far."

"What are you talking about?"

"The die is cast, little brother."

Wordlessly I walked with him to the chopper field and saw but couldn't hear him talking to the pilot of one of the Hueys we had flown in before. I was more afraid that moment than at any time during the two tours we had spent here.

We were a half-hour north of the base when I saw the three evenly spaced bullet holes appear in the side of the helicopter next to the door. Patty was sitting on his phone book between me and the open door. His body jerked slightly toward me, and my heart stopped beating. I felt a gut-wrenching chill as every drop of blood seemed to drain from my face. Using his heels to push himself, he twisted to face me. He was biting his lower lip, and for the first time in my life I saw tears in my brother's eyes. He wasn't afraid, but he was crying.

A great emptiness filled me. A loneliness that I had never felt left me cold, and I shuddered. He half-smiled and said, "They didn't get my balls did they, brother?" He held his hands on his chest, and the bright red blood seeped around his fingers and fell to the dirty floor of the helicopter like red wine. Each drop of his life glistened there for a second, bright red, then turned the color of umber. He must have been reading my mind.

"Looks just like wine, don't it, boy? I hope this is a good year for it." I nodded my head because I couldn't speak. He had quit smiling now. "Matty, I'm going to be meeting our mamma and I'm going to tell her what a fine man you grew up to be and I'm going to tell her how much I love you. Now if you don't mind I'd like for you to hold my hand because I'm never again going to see the leaves you call October's blood again." I held him and cried until a long time after his blood wasn't red anymore. Half of me was gone forever.

When the helicopter landed, an army ambulance was waiting. Medics pried my hands away and took him. The helicopter's blades finally quit their swish and were silent now. Everything was uncommonly silent. A lone crow flew over us low and cawed. It landed on a sagging temporary power line and bobbed its head and cawed again. It was the saddest sound I had ever heard.

I left Vietnam the next day and flew to Albany to wait for the casket that held my brother's remains. I would follow the military escort to the cemetery where my mother and father were buried and where we would bury Patty. I felt as if I couldn't lift my left arm anymore. I felt as if part of me was in that casket somewhere in the belly of a cargo plane.

I don't know how she knew I was coming, but she knew, and she was there when the plane landed. A tall chain-link fence separated spectators from the passenger unloading area, and I saw her with her hands high and gripping the diamond-shaped mesh of the fence. She looked more mature, far more beautiful than she'd ever been, quieter, more sure of herself. Her first words were "Matty, I've got cheerleader practice tonight, and I asked my mother if maybe you could go with me because I don't know how to change a flat tire."

I said, "Leighanne, I can't. He's dead."

"I know. Aunt Hattie told me."

"Is that how you knew when I came home last time?"

"You don't know much about women, do you, Matty?"

I didn't answer. "I've talked to Aunt Hattie at least once a week since that New Year's Day years ago."

She stayed with me that night and cried with me and finally at dawn we both slept. Late that afternoon I lifted the pillow she had used to cover her head. "Leighanne, I don't think I can live without you. I need you to help me bury my brother."

"Take my word for it, Matty, you can't. Nor can I live without you. God knows I've tried hard enough."

The ambulance picked up my brother the next morning. Leighanne and I followed it through the countryside toward the plantation and Macedonia church where Patty would be buried. An olive-green sedan with four soldiers in dress uniform followed behind our car. When the sergeant in charge gave the other three the order, they would raise their rifles and each would shoot seven times toward heaven. Then we would bury my best friend.

When we drove by the place where the Plantation Sportsman's Club had been, I saw a new building that looked almost like the old club, only more dingy. Across the front in bold letters was a sign that said "Bunk's Place—Bunk Bartlet, proprietor." Several pickup trucks were parked at random angles in front of the building. A pyramid of empty beer cans six feet high was positioned on one end of the building like a monument to depravity. Memories of all the things that had happened seemed to focus inside me, and I felt a rage toward that building.

When the funeral was over and everyone had left the cemetery, I stayed and sat with Patty for several hours. Uncle Charlie sat with me for a while, then I asked him to go. I told Patty goodbye for the last time and walked down the little sandy lane to the main road. When we had gotten there, the church yard and both sides of the narrow road leading to the church were filled with cars, so Leighanne had parked beside the main road. She was waiting, and I apologized for taking so long. She drove to the lake, the place we had met so many times, the place where I had told her I loved her a thousand years ago.

I asked her to marry me and she said, "Yes, but first I want you to meet a couple of little people that you really need to know."

I asked who they were, and she said that they were twins and three months old and the oldest was named John Matthew MacDonald II, after his father, and the youngest was named James Patrick MacDonald II, after his uncle. I asked her what the hell she was talking about, and she said, "Matty, it's a generally accepted fact that fish is a brain food, and I know that you don't eat fish, but you figure it out."

As Yogi Berra said, "This sounds like déjà vu all over again."

I wondered if Uncle Charlie might want to raise two

more. When we drove back to the main house, Nate and Chief were waiting. I suppose they knew this is where I'd come. I hadn't talked to either of the men since last year when I was home on leave.

Nate nodded to Leighanne then turned to me. "Chief and myself found out who killed Press."

"Was it Bunk or one of those bastards who hang out with him?"

"Yep. One of his friends."

"Where is he now?"

Chief answered. "The last time we saw him, and I don't think he's gone anywhere, we left him resting in the middle of Chickasawhatchee Swamp."

Nate spoke. "I guess you saw that Bunk rebuilt the beer joint."

"I saw it."

He looked over his shoulder at the sun. "I spoke to Mr. Bickerstaff at the funeral. He said we could borrow his truck again. I guess me and Chief could get them bulls loaded up in about an hour."

I looked at Leighanne. She raised her head slightly, and I saw the faintest of smiles. "I'll go get the boys while you're gone."

As Uncle Charlie would say, "If my granddaddy was alive, he would turn over in his grave. Man, this calls for an orgasm."

Epilogue

I AM PROBABLY THE LUCKIEST MAN ON EARTH TO HAVE LIVED how and when I did and to have loved and had the love of so many special people. Leighanne taught me what a heart was for, and I truly believe she got what she wanted out of life. The Colonel taught me values, ethics, a sense of proprietorship, respect for the land, and so much more. Uncle Charlie showed me wisdom, in a weird way. Nate and Chief showed me the mother we call nature. Aunt Hattie pointed out goodness and right. My brother showed me all the rest.

The boys are almost grown now and spend a great deal of time trying to drive Nate and Chief crazy. I often walk down the sandy road to the small white church nestled half-hidden in the live oaks. I sit on the gray coping that forms a square around the headstones, now four, and I listen to the birds chirping and fussing in the trees or watch the hawks riding high and easy on unseen thermals that provide the wind beneath their wings. I watch the wavelike motions of the golden broom sedge as the quaking, rolling, waist-high plants seem to lap toward some familiar shore.

Aunt Hattie left an empty place in my life a few years back, and Uncle Charlie likes to sit in the warm sunshine now and talk of things that were and things that should be and things that will never be.

The left side of the wide headstone already has my name and date of birth in place. It lacks a final date. Someday, when my heart quits hurting, I will tell you the rest of the story.